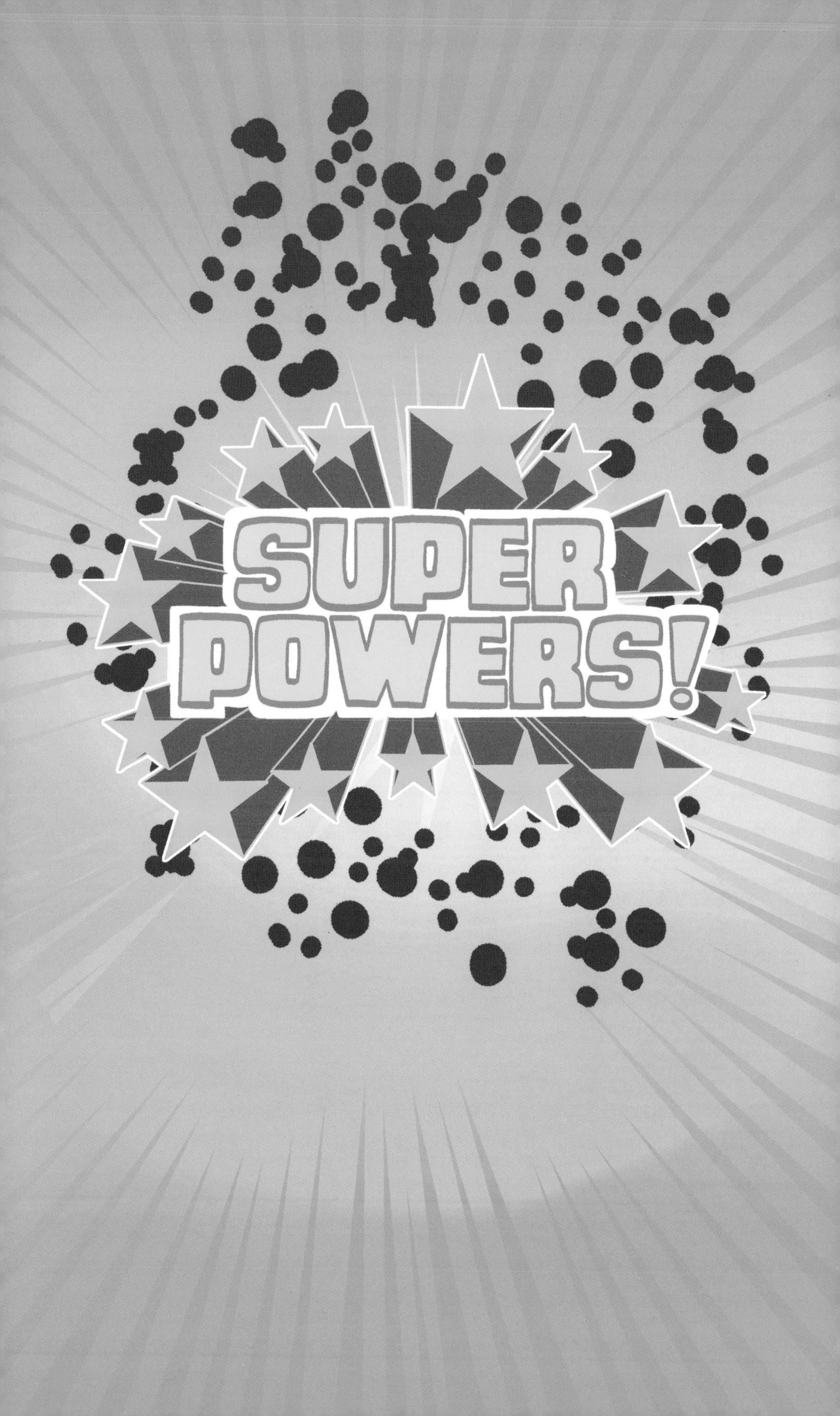
SUPER
POWERS!

Super Powers! is published by
Stone Arch Books,
A Capstone Imprint
1710 Roe Crest Drive
North Mankato, Minnesota 56003
www.mycapstone.com

Cataloging-in-Publication Data is available at the Library of Congress website:
ISBN: 978-1-4965-7398-8 (library binding)
ISBN: 978-1-4965-7404-6 (eBook PDF)

Summary: The Legion of Doom battles the Justice League! What team will win, what team will lose, and WHAT is that strange giant starfish?

STONE ARCH BOOKS
Chris Harbo Editorial Director
Gena Chester Editor
Hilary Wacholz Art Director
Kris Wilfahrt Production Specialist

Superman created by Jerry Siegel and Joe Shuster. By special arrangement with the Jerry Siegel family.

Printed in the United States.
PA021

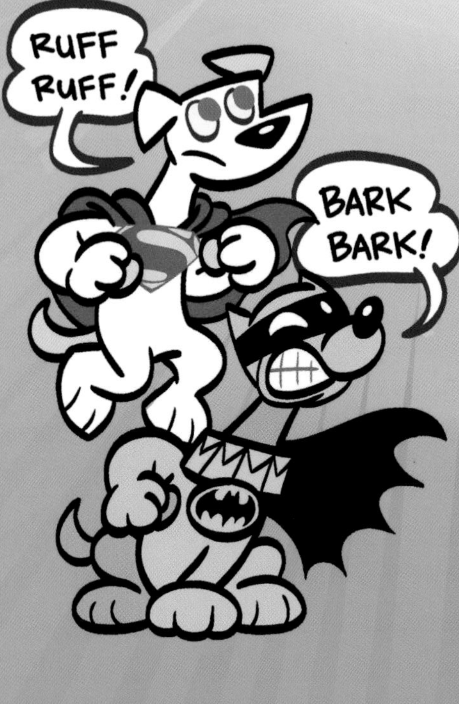
RUFF RUFF!
BARK BARK!

SUPER POWERS!

League vs. Legion!

BY ART BALTAZAR AND FRANCO

STONE ARCH BOOKS
a capstone imprint

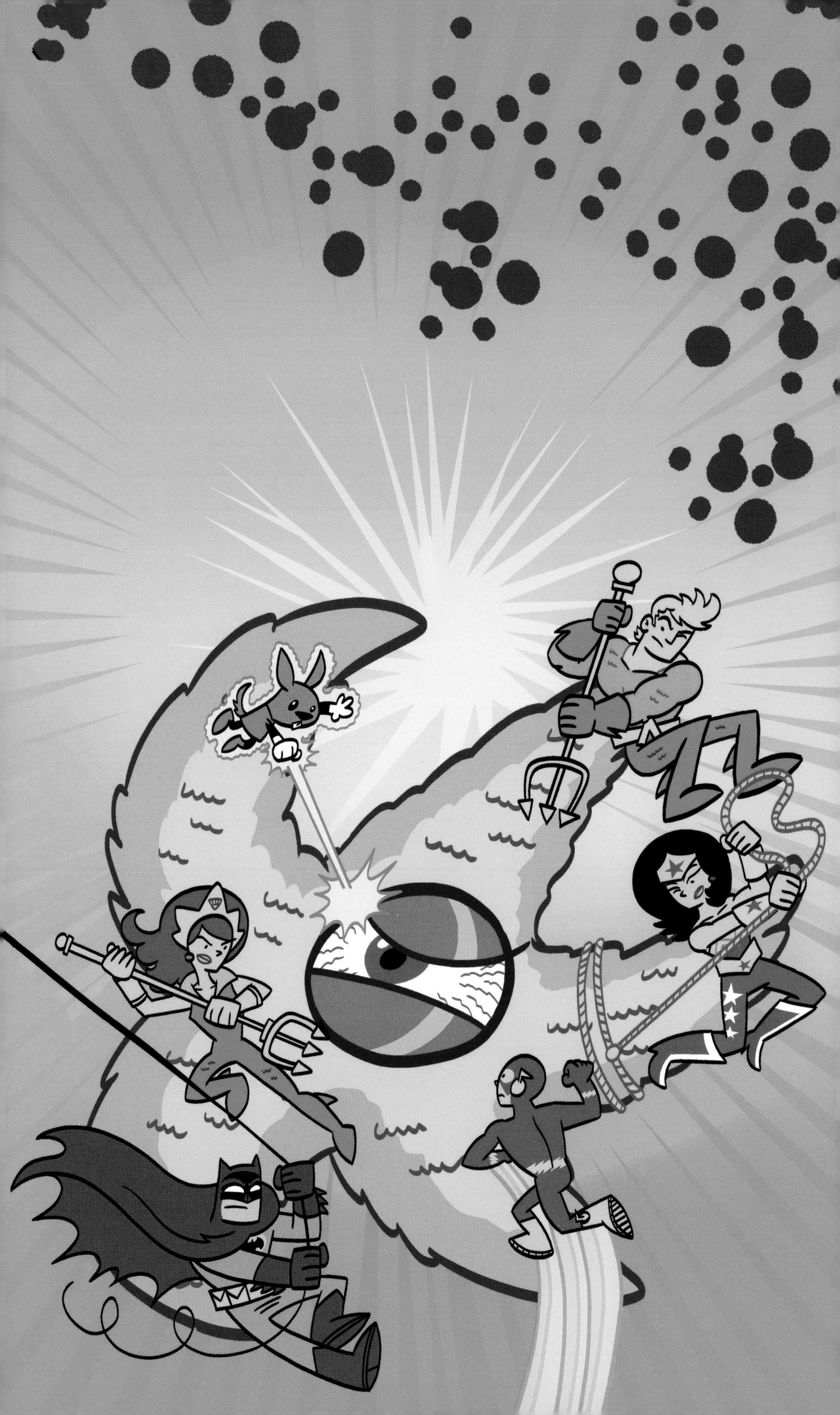

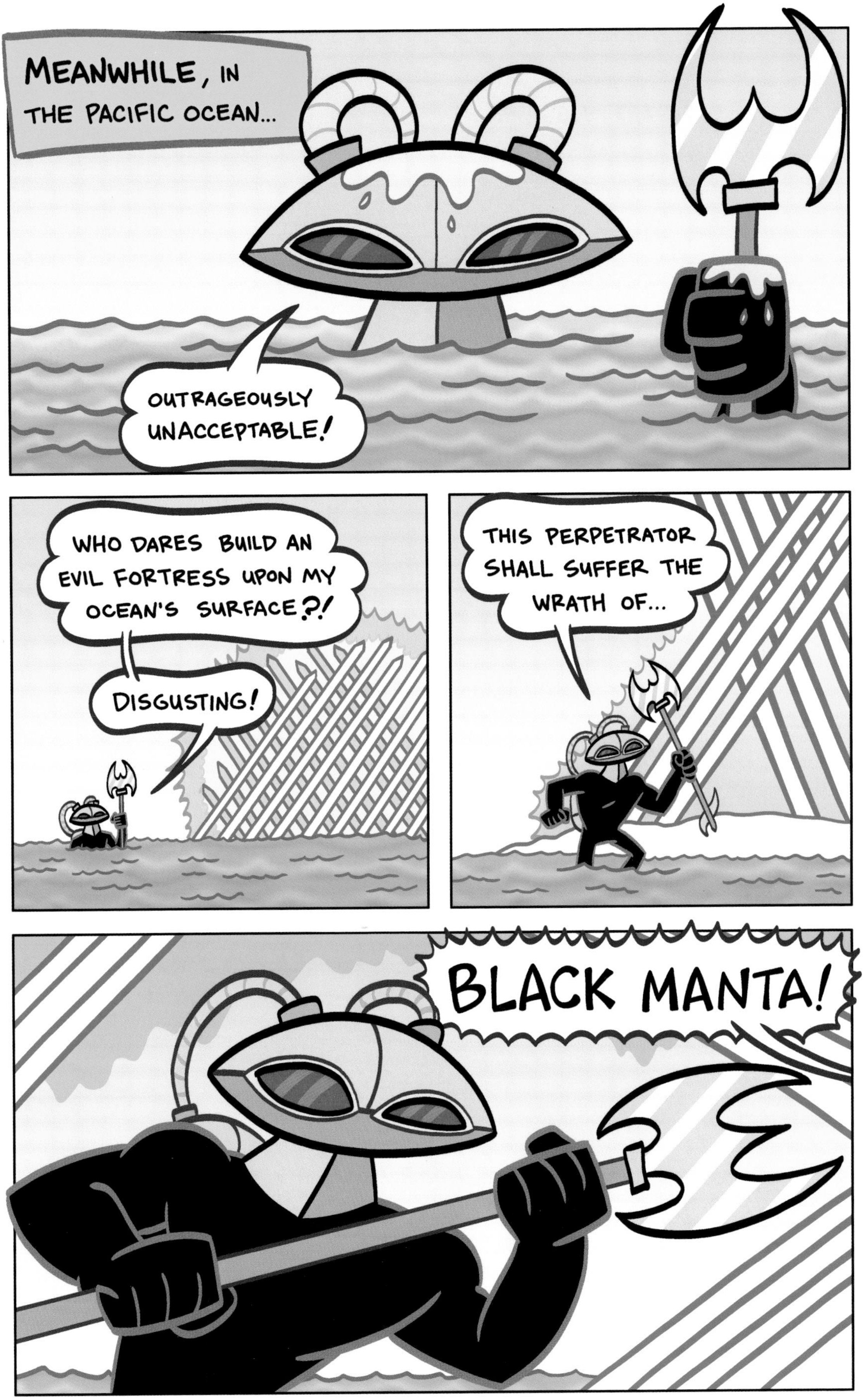
MEANWHILE, IN THE PACIFIC OCEAN...
OUTRAGEOUSLY UNACCEPTABLE!
WHO DARES BUILD AN EVIL FORTRESS UPON MY OCEAN'S SURFACE?!
DISGUSTING!
THIS PERPETRATOR SHALL SUFFER THE WRATH OF...
BLACK MANTA!

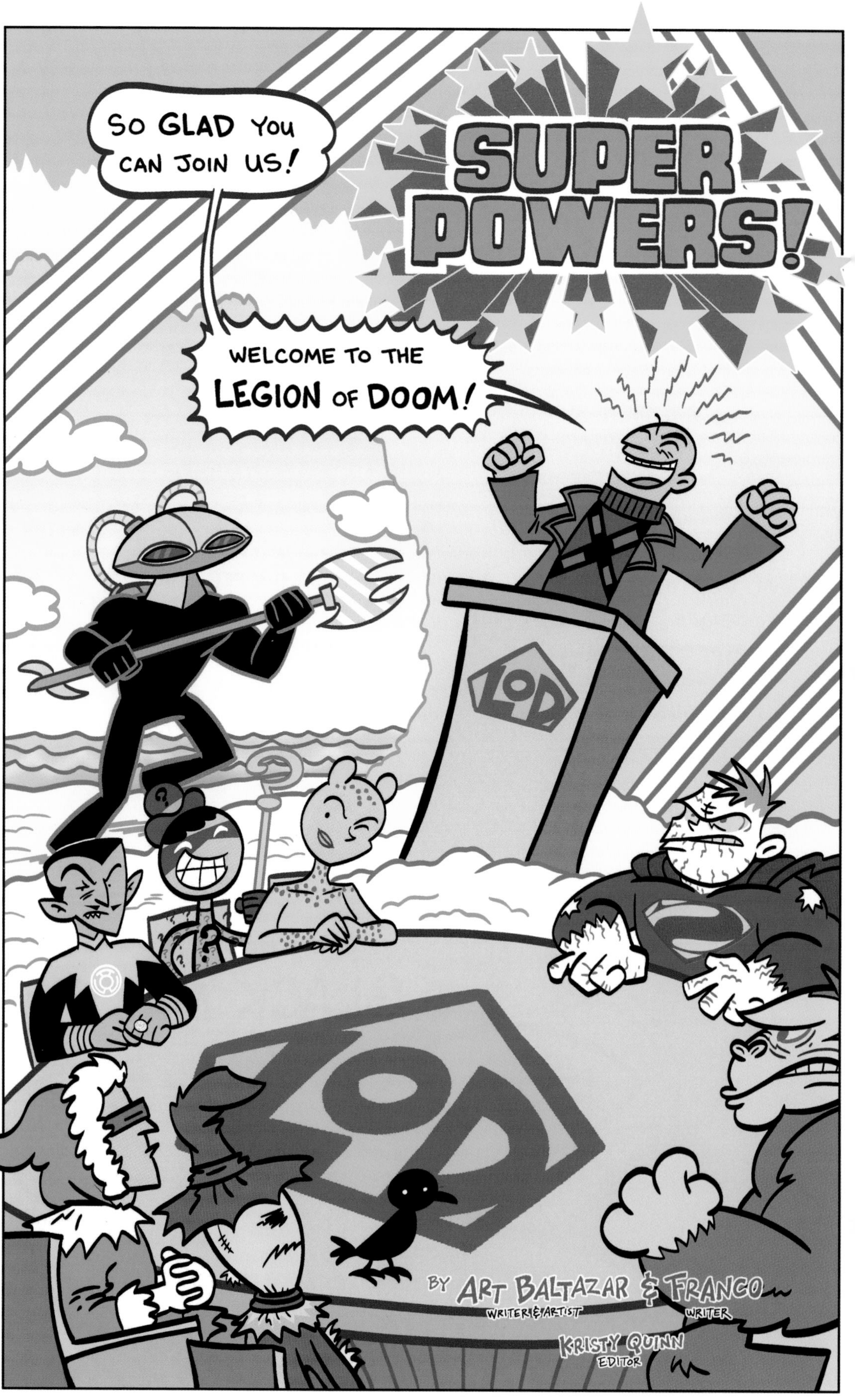
SO GLAD YOU CAN JOIN US!
WELCOME TO THE LEGION OF DOOM!
SUPER POWERS!
L.O.D.
BY ART BALTAZAR & FRANCO
WRITER & ARTIST
WRITER
KRISTY QUINN
EDITOR

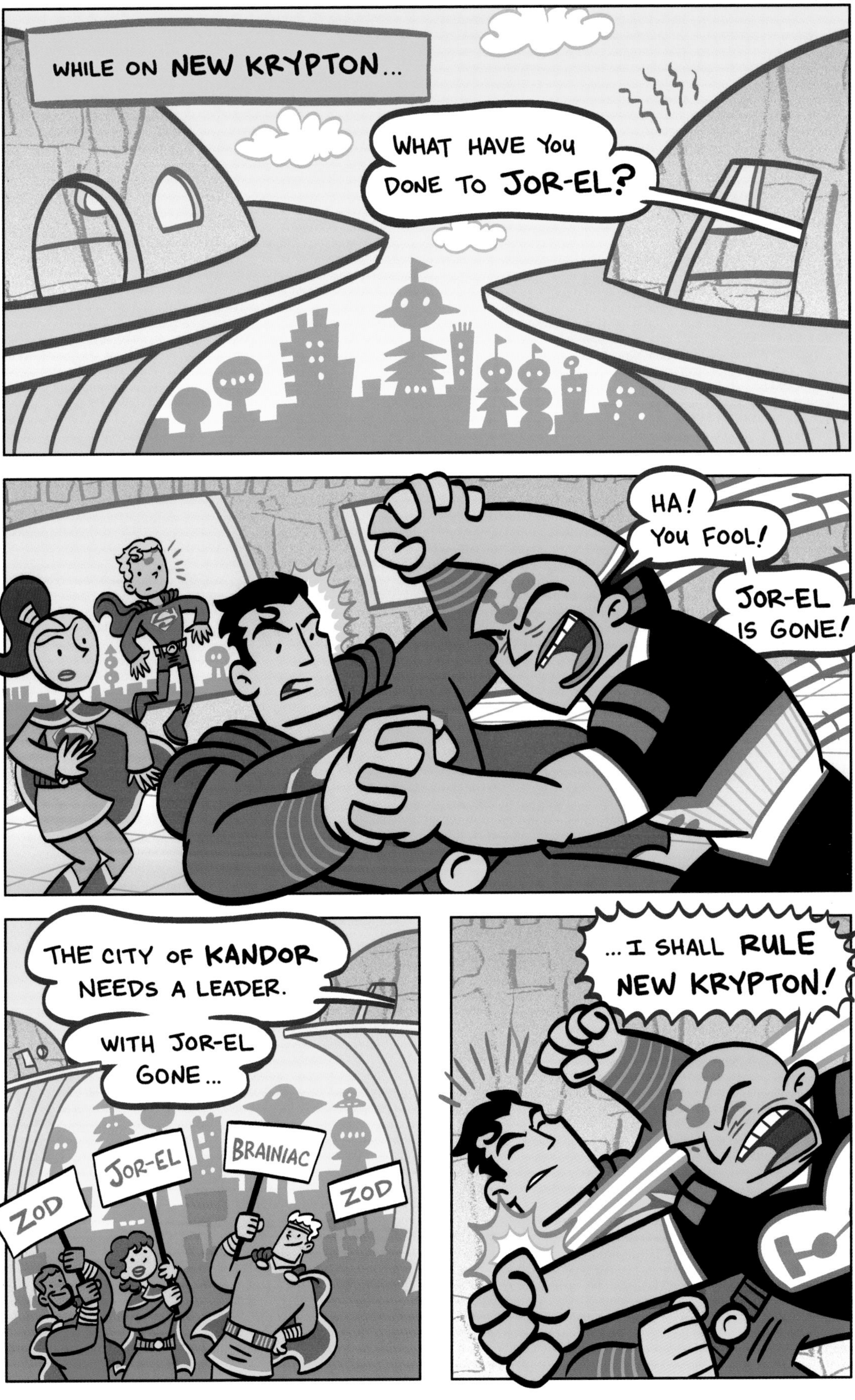
WHILE ON NEW KRYPTON...
WHAT HAVE YOU DONE TO JOR-EL?
HA! YOU FOOL!
JOR-EL IS GONE!
THE CITY OF KANDOR NEEDS A LEADER.
WITH JOR-EL GONE...
ZOD
JOR-EL
BRAINIAC
ZOD
...I SHALL RULE NEW KRYPTON!

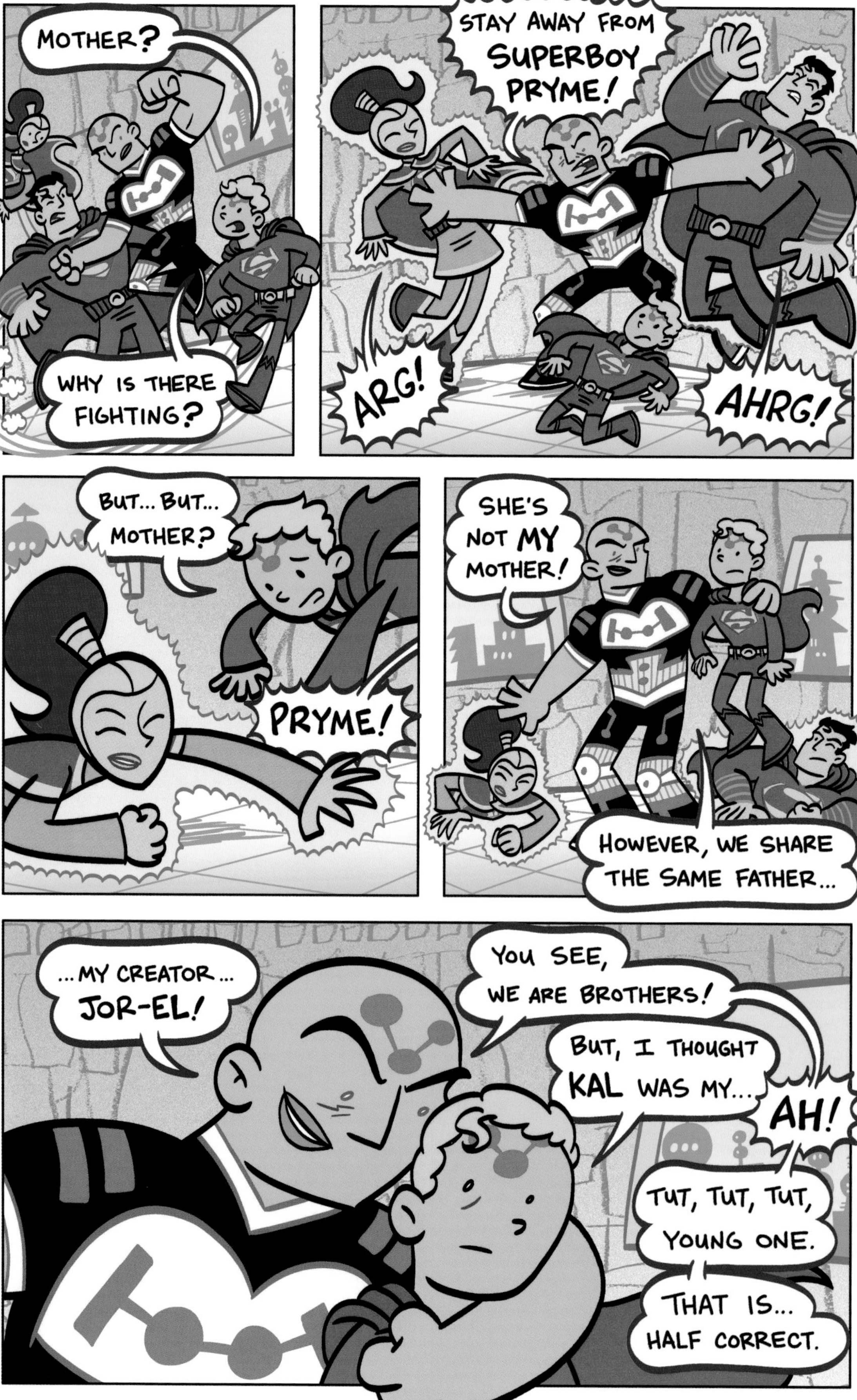
MOTHER?
WHY IS THERE FIGHTING?
STAY AWAY FROM SUPERBOY PRYME!
ARG!
AHRG!
BUT... BUT... MOTHER?
PRYME!
SHE'S NOT MY MOTHER!
HOWEVER, WE SHARE THE SAME FATHER...
...MY CREATOR... JOR-EL!
YOU SEE, WE ARE BROTHERS!
BUT, I THOUGHT KAL WAS MY...
AH!
TUT, TUT, TUT, YOUNG ONE.
THAT IS... HALF CORRECT.

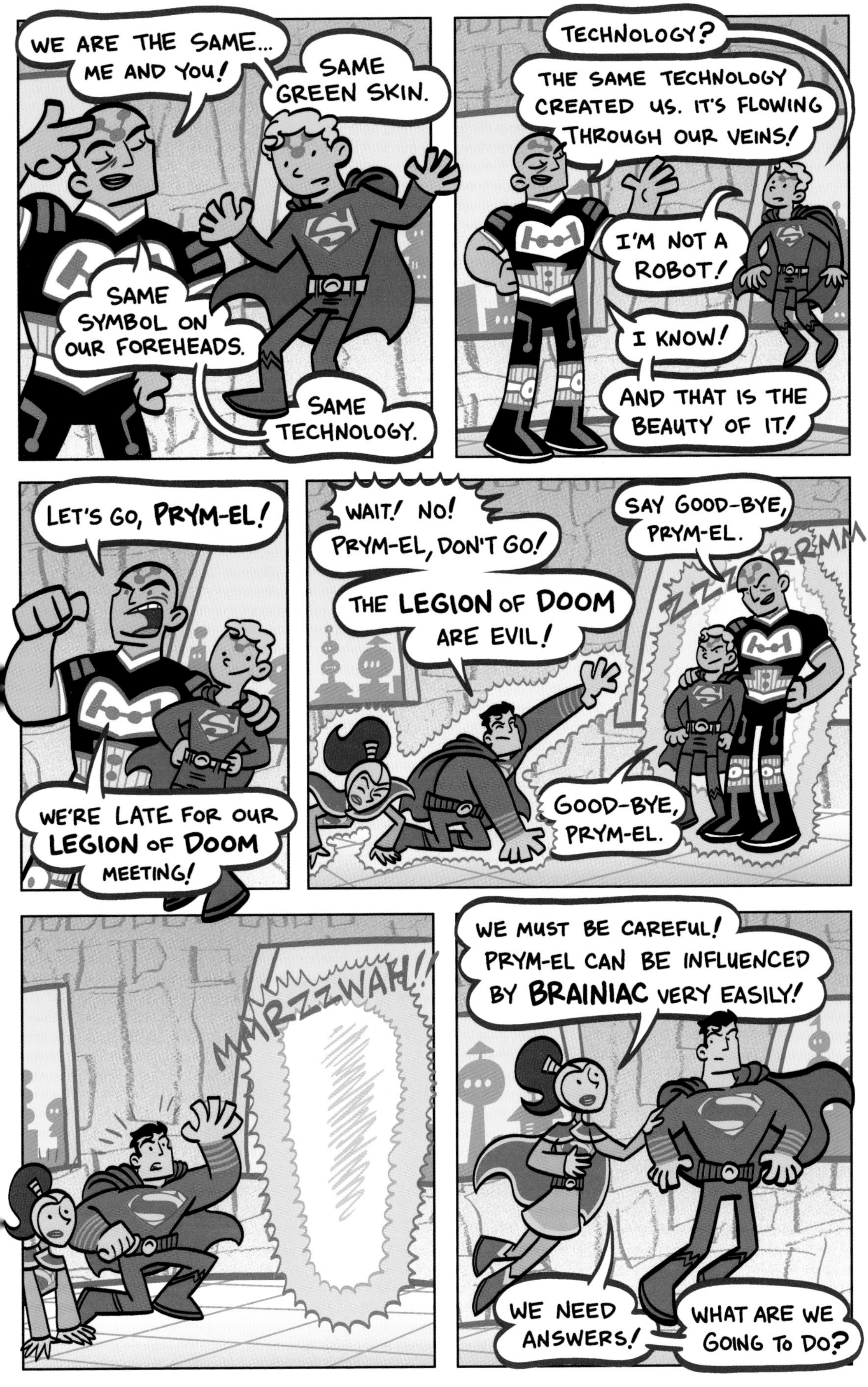
WE ARE THE SAME... ME AND YOU!
SAME GREEN SKIN.
SAME SYMBOL ON OUR FOREHEADS.
SAME TECHNOLOGY.
TECHNOLOGY?
THE SAME TECHNOLOGY CREATED US. IT'S FLOWING THROUGH OUR VEINS!
I'M NOT A ROBOT!
I KNOW!
AND THAT IS THE BEAUTY OF IT!
LET'S GO, PRYM-EL!
WE'RE LATE FOR OUR LEGION OF DOOM MEETING!
WAIT! NO! PRYM-EL, DON'T GO!
THE LEGION OF DOOM ARE EVIL!
SAY GOOD-BYE, PRYM-EL.
ZZZZRRMM
GOOD-BYE, PRYM-EL.
MMRZZWAH!!
WE MUST BE CAREFUL! PRYM-EL CAN BE INFLUENCED BY BRAINIAC VERY EASILY!
WE NEED ANSWERS!
WHAT ARE WE GOING TO DO?

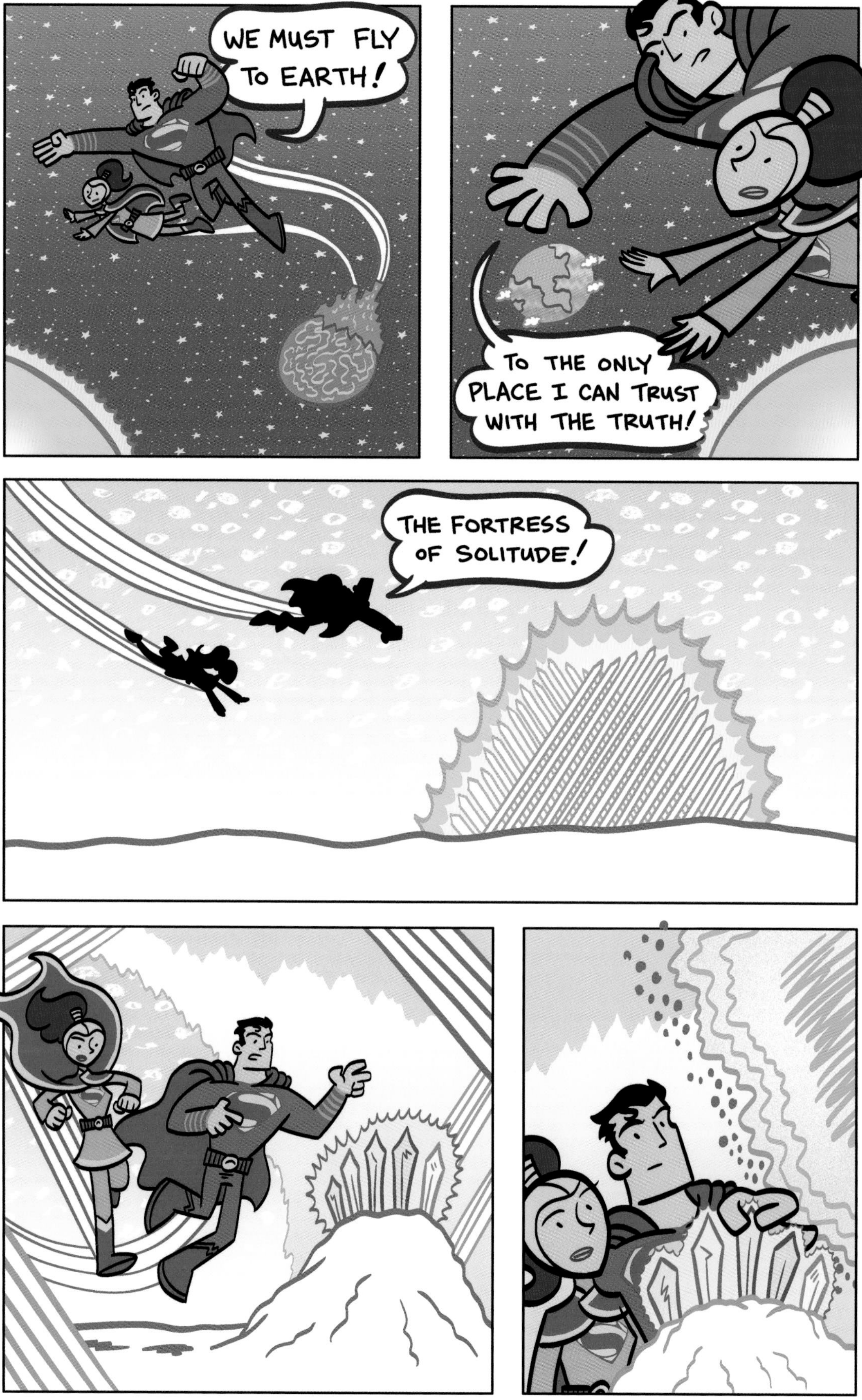
WE MUST FLY TO EARTH!
TO THE ONLY PLACE I CAN TRUST WITH THE TRUTH!
THE FORTRESS OF SOLITUDE!

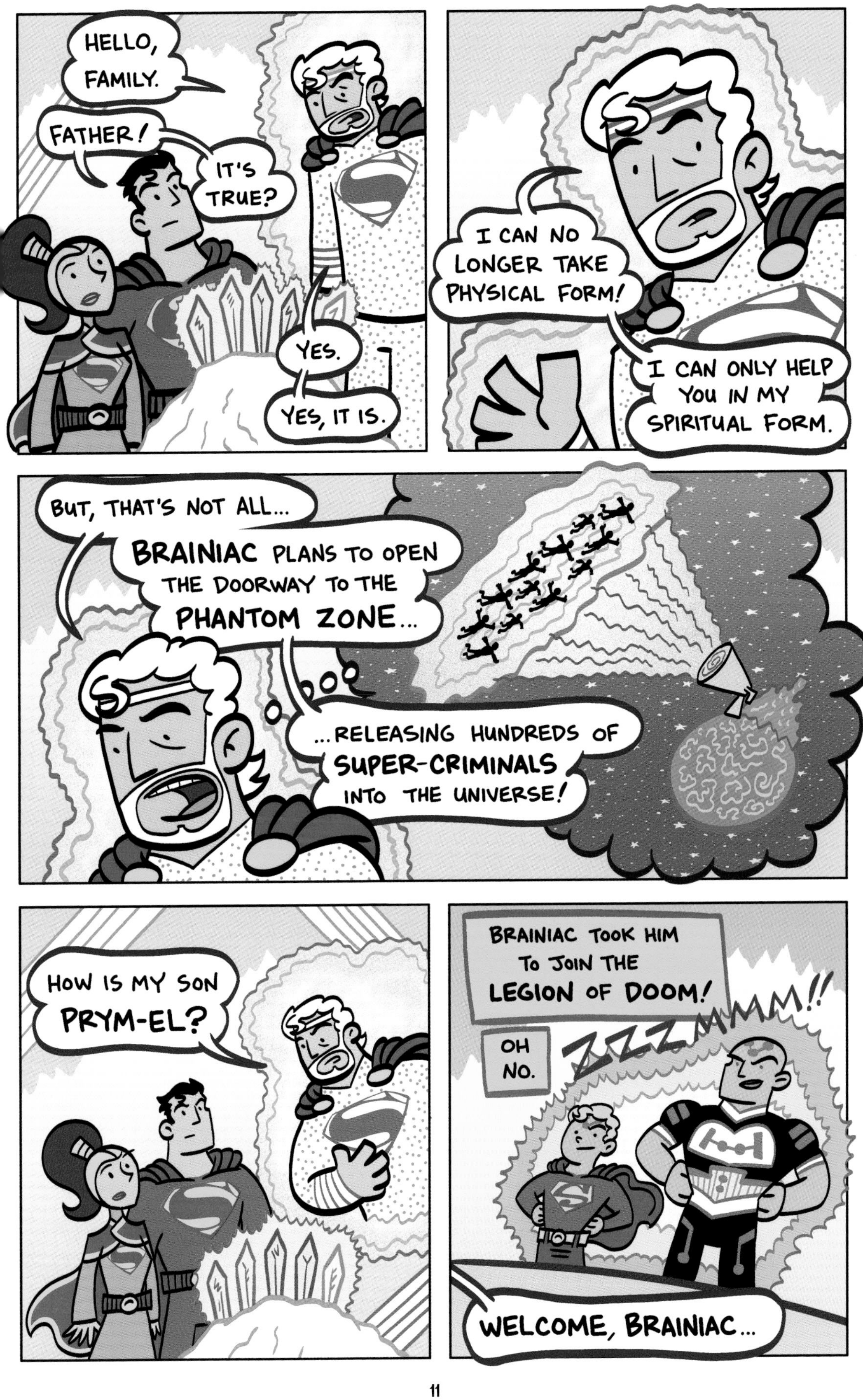

HELLO, FAMILY.
FATHER!
IT'S TRUE?
YES.
YES, IT IS.
I CAN NO LONGER TAKE PHYSICAL FORM!
I CAN ONLY HELP YOU IN MY SPIRITUAL FORM.
BUT, THAT'S NOT ALL...
BRAINIAC PLANS TO OPEN THE DOORWAY TO THE PHANTOM ZONE...
...RELEASING HUNDREDS OF SUPER-CRIMINALS INTO THE UNIVERSE!
HOW IS MY SON PRYM-EL?
BRAINIAC TOOK HIM TO JOIN THE LEGION OF DOOM!
OH NO.
ZZZZMMMM!!
WELCOME, BRAINIAC...

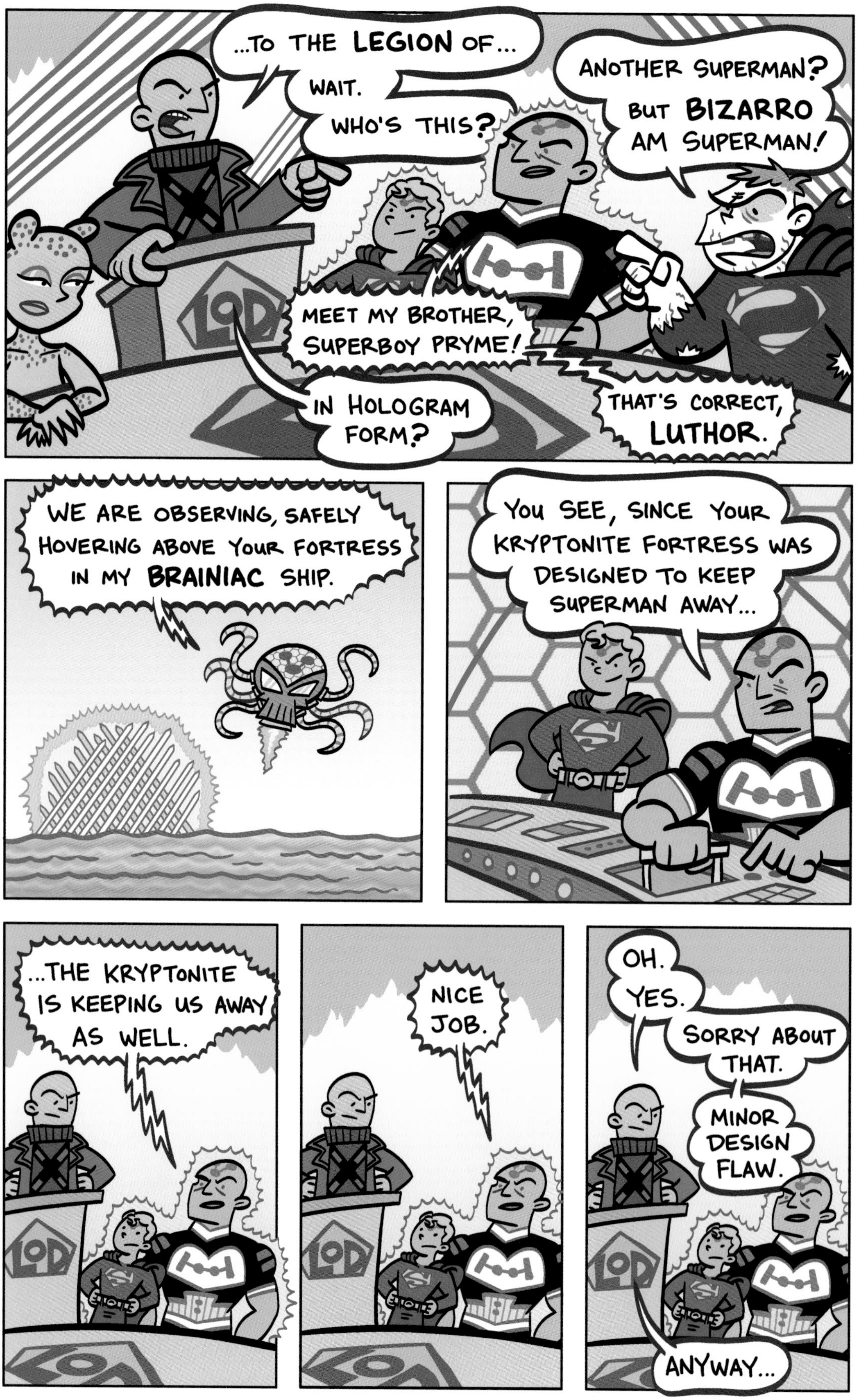
...TO THE LEGION OF...
WAIT.
WHO'S THIS?
ANOTHER SUPERMAN?
BUT BIZARRO AM SUPERMAN!
MEET MY BROTHER, SUPERBOY PRYME!
IN HOLOGRAM FORM?
THAT'S CORRECT, LUTHOR.
WE ARE OBSERVING, SAFELY HOVERING ABOVE YOUR FORTRESS IN MY BRAINIAC SHIP.
YOU SEE, SINCE YOUR KRYPTONITE FORTRESS WAS DESIGNED TO KEEP SUPERMAN AWAY...
...THE KRYPTONITE IS KEEPING US AWAY AS WELL.
NICE JOB.
OH.
YES.
SORRY ABOUT THAT.
MINOR DESIGN FLAW.
ANYWAY...

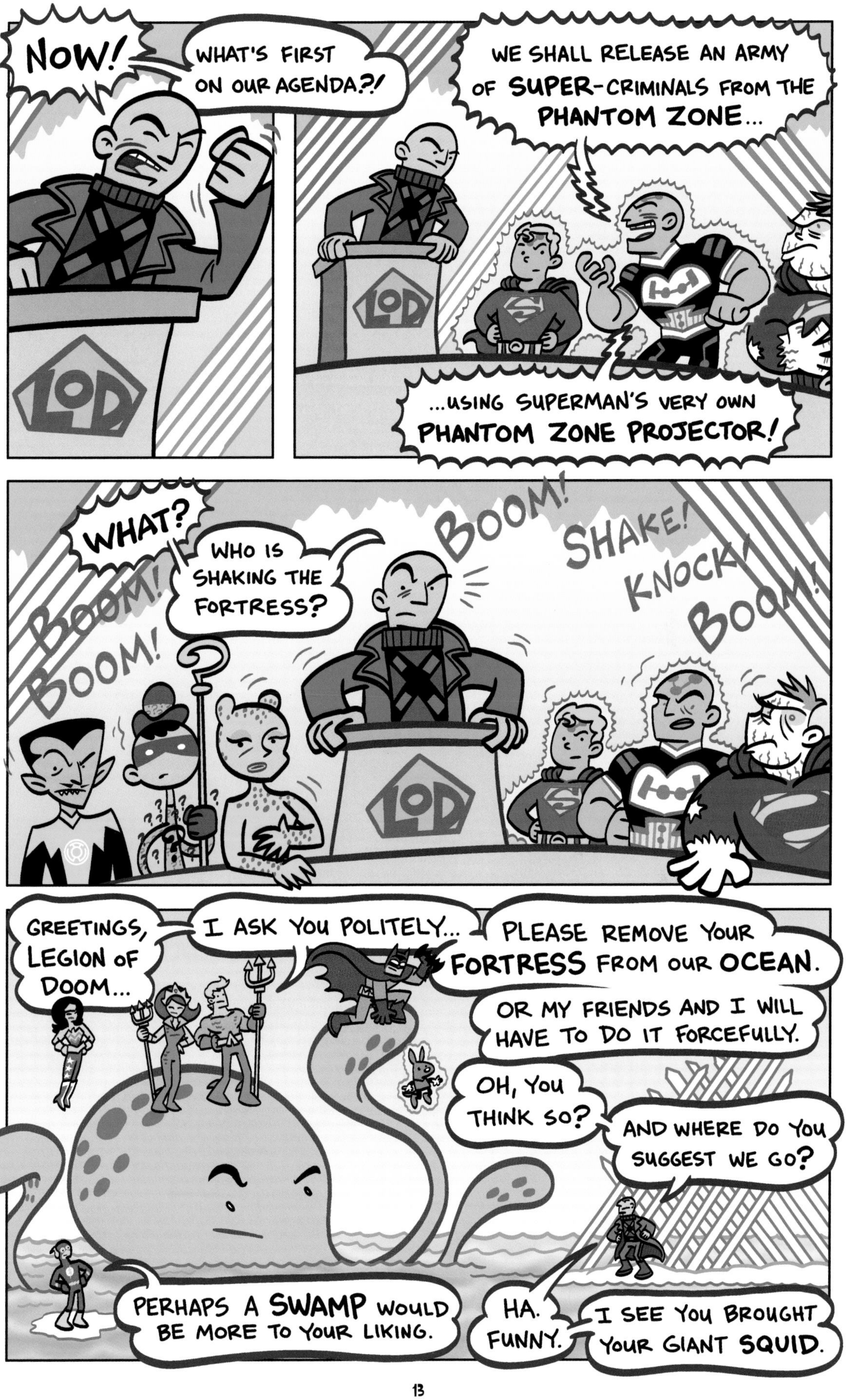
NOW!
WHAT'S FIRST ON OUR AGENDA?!
WE SHALL RELEASE AN ARMY OF SUPER-CRIMINALS FROM THE PHANTOM ZONE...
...USING SUPERMAN'S VERY OWN PHANTOM ZONE PROJECTOR!
WHAT?
WHO IS SHAKING THE FORTRESS?
BOOM!
BOOM!
BOOM!
SHAKE!
KNOCK!
BOOM!
GREETINGS, LEGION OF DOOM...
I ASK YOU POLITELY...
PLEASE REMOVE YOUR FORTRESS FROM OUR OCEAN.
OR MY FRIENDS AND I WILL HAVE TO DO IT FORCEFULLY.
OH, YOU THINK SO?
AND WHERE DO YOU SUGGEST WE GO?
PERHAPS A SWAMP WOULD BE MORE TO YOUR LIKING.
HA. FUNNY.
I SEE YOU BROUGHT YOUR GIANT SQUID.

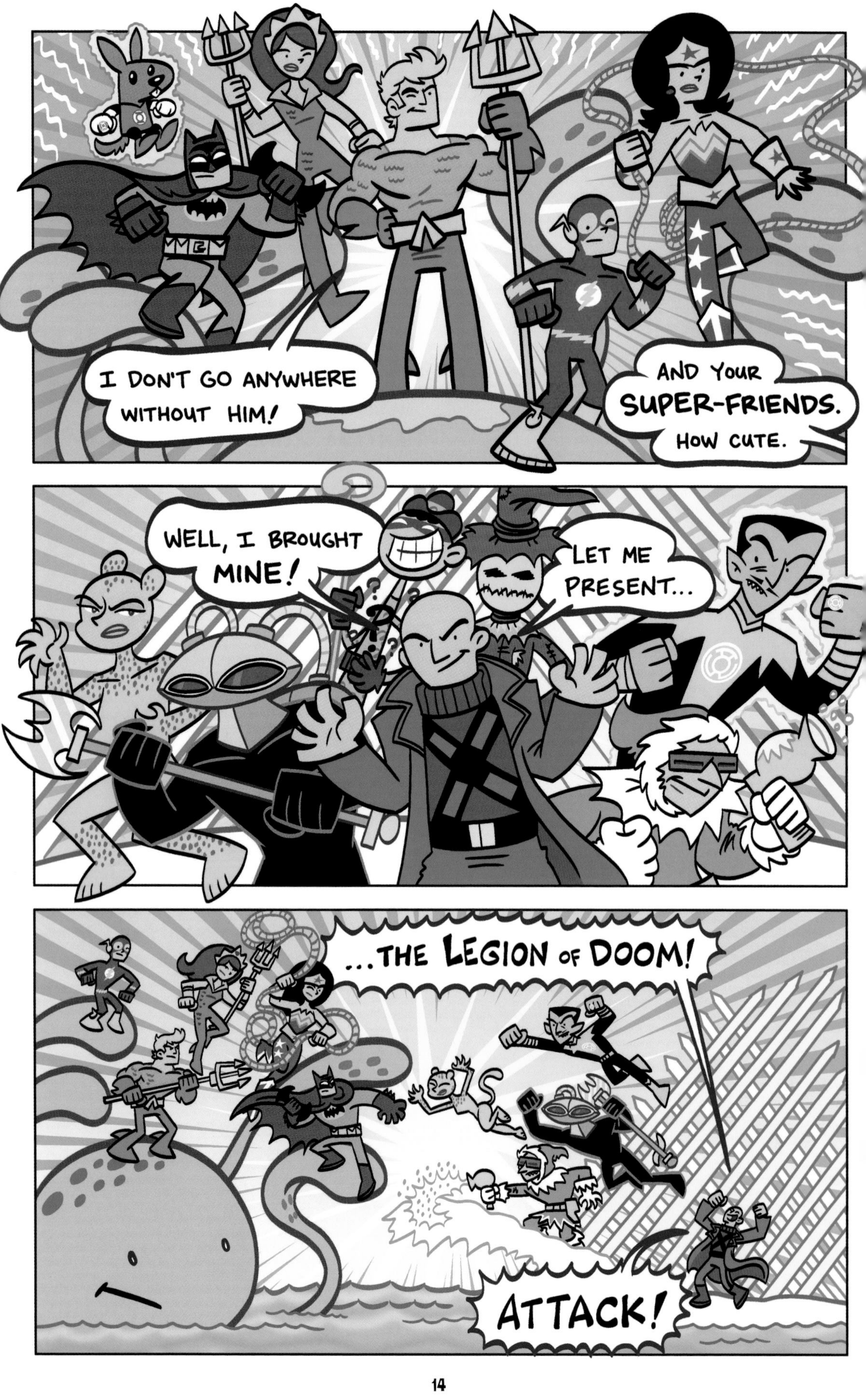
I DON'T GO ANYWHERE WITHOUT HIM!
AND YOUR SUPER-FRIENDS. HOW CUTE.
WELL, I BROUGHT MINE!
LET ME PRESENT...
...THE LEGION OF DOOM!
ATTACK!

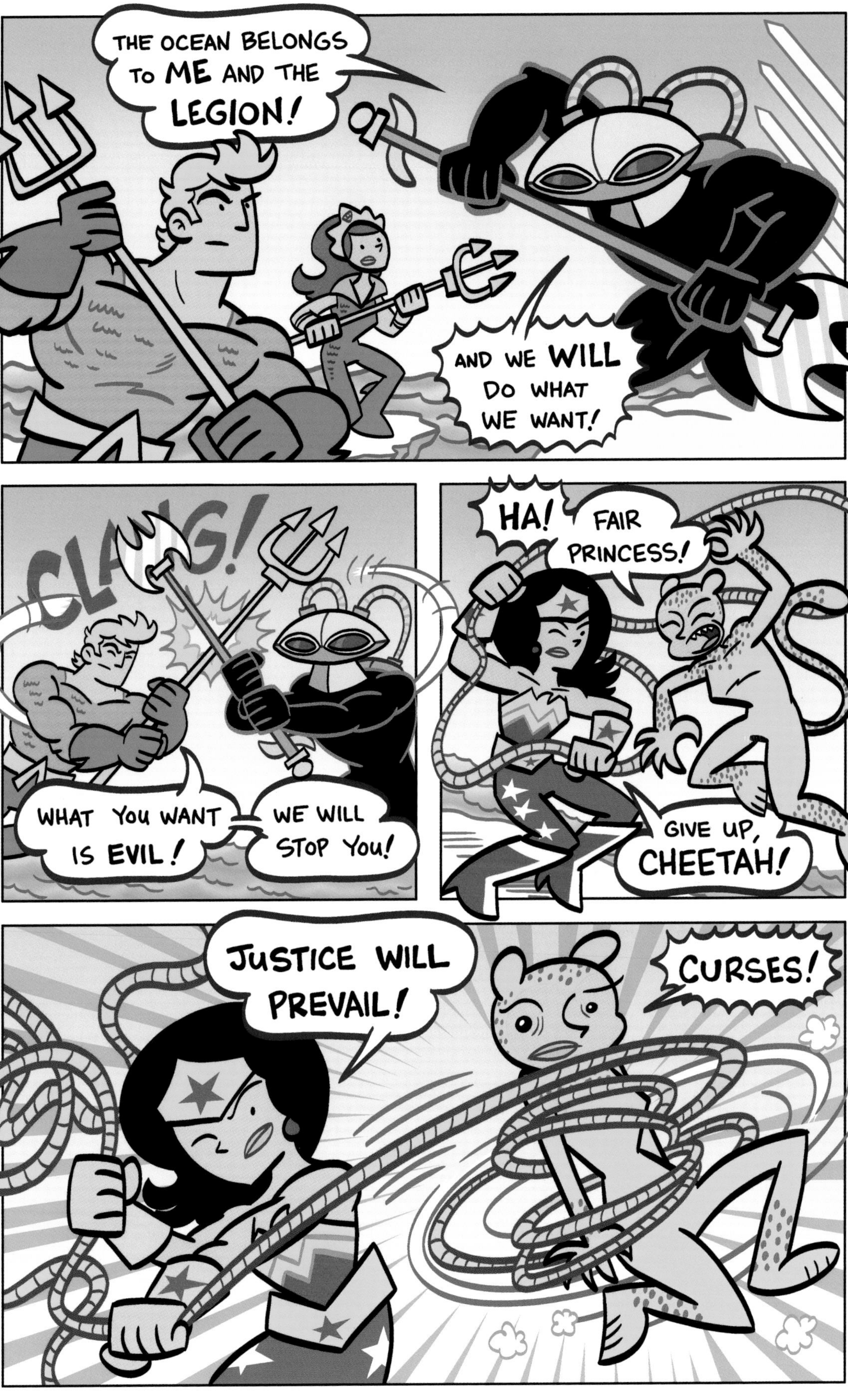
THE OCEAN BELONGS TO ME AND THE LEGION!
AND WE WILL DO WHAT WE WANT!
CLANG!
WHAT YOU WANT IS EVIL!
WE WILL STOP YOU!
HA!
FAIR PRINCESS!
GIVE UP, CHEETAH!
JUSTICE WILL PREVAIL!
CURSES!

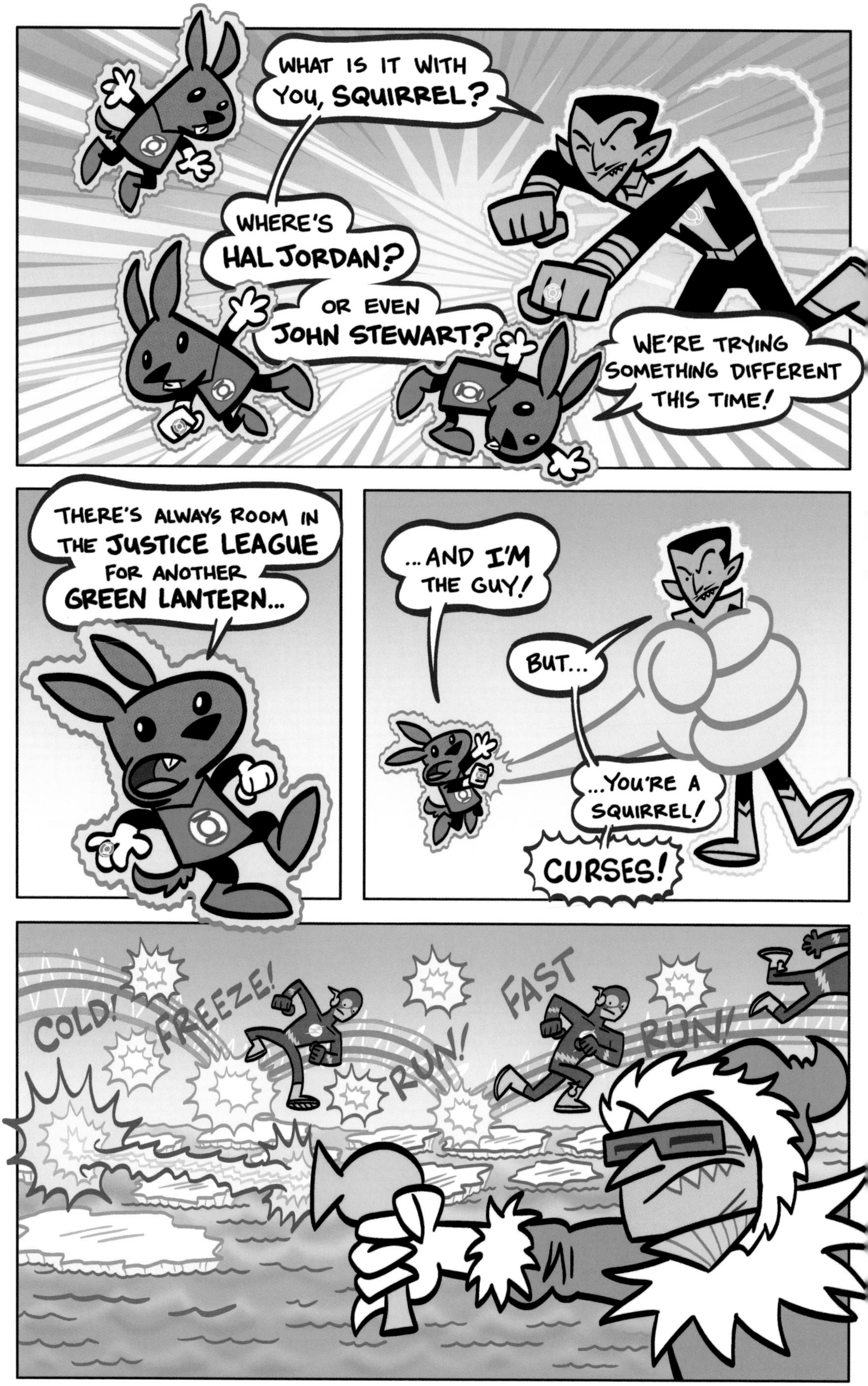
WHAT IS IT WITH YOU, SQUIRREL?
WHERE'S HAL JORDAN?
OR EVEN JOHN STEWART?
WE'RE TRYING SOMETHING DIFFERENT THIS TIME!
THERE'S ALWAYS ROOM IN THE JUSTICE LEAGUE FOR ANOTHER GREEN LANTERN...
...AND I'M THE GUY!
BUT...
...YOU'RE A SQUIRREL!
CURSES!
COLD!
FREEZE!
RUN!
FAST
RUN!

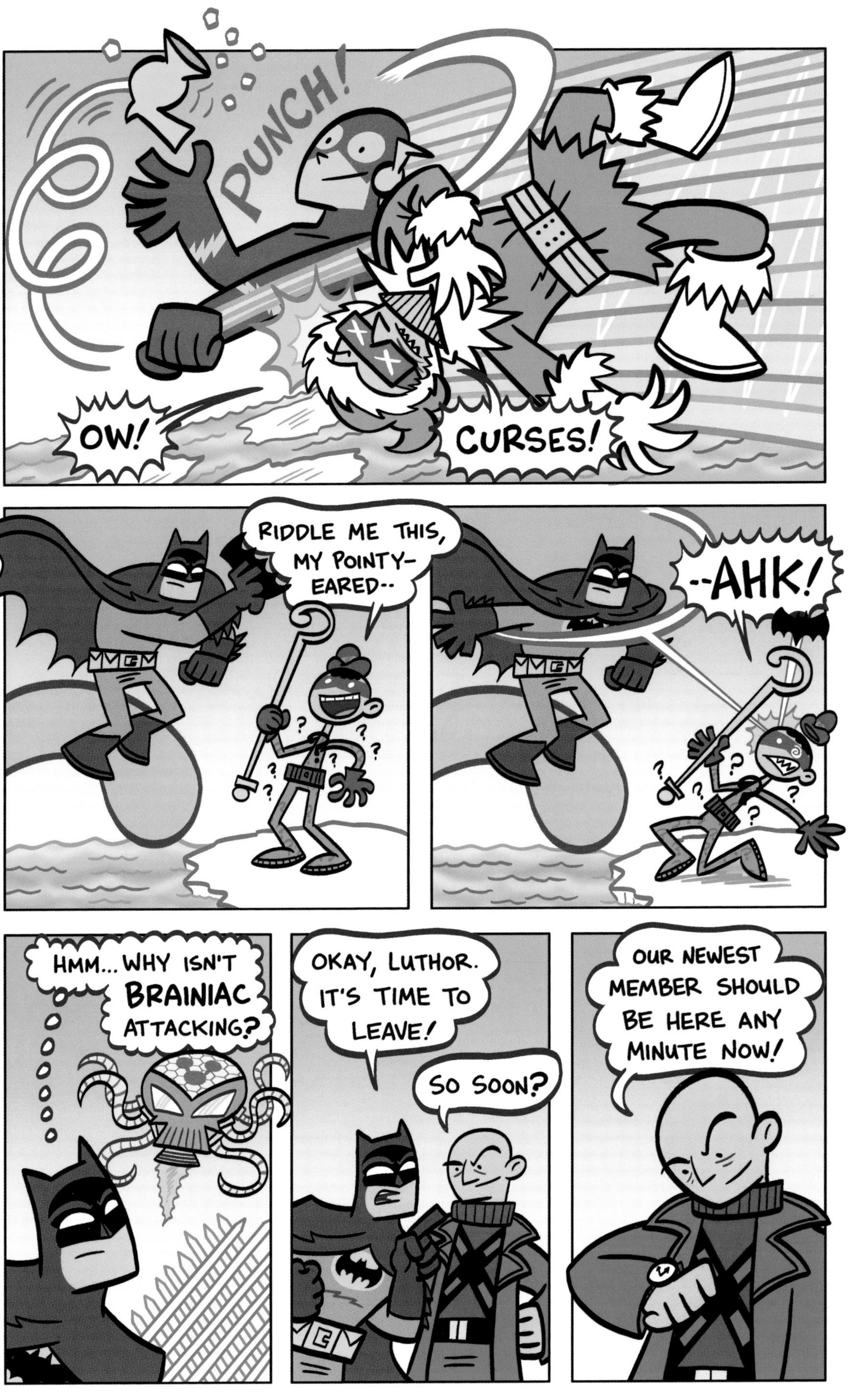
PUNCH!
OW!
CURSES!
RIDDLE ME THIS, MY POINTY-EARED--
--AHK!
HMM... WHY ISN'T BRAINIAC ATTACKING?
OKAY, LUTHOR. IT'S TIME TO LEAVE!
SO SOON?
OUR NEWEST MEMBER SHOULD BE HERE ANY MINUTE NOW!

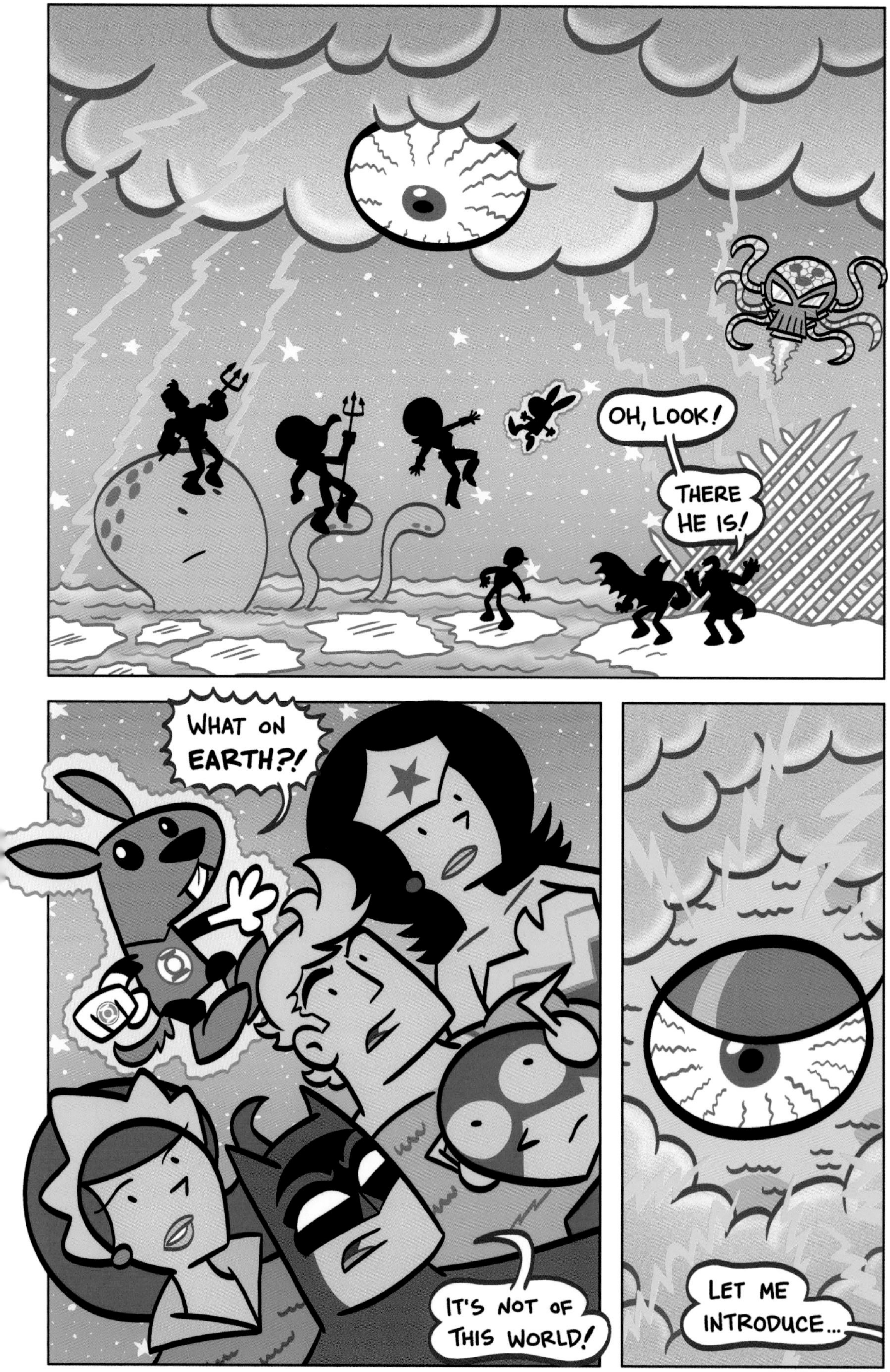
OH, LOOK!
THERE HE IS!
WHAT ON EARTH?!
IT'S NOT OF THIS WORLD!
LET ME INTRODUCE...

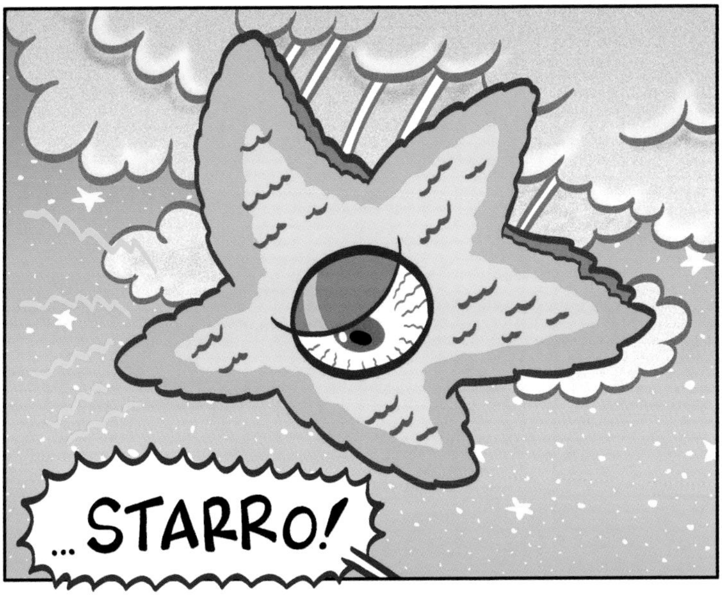
...STARRO!

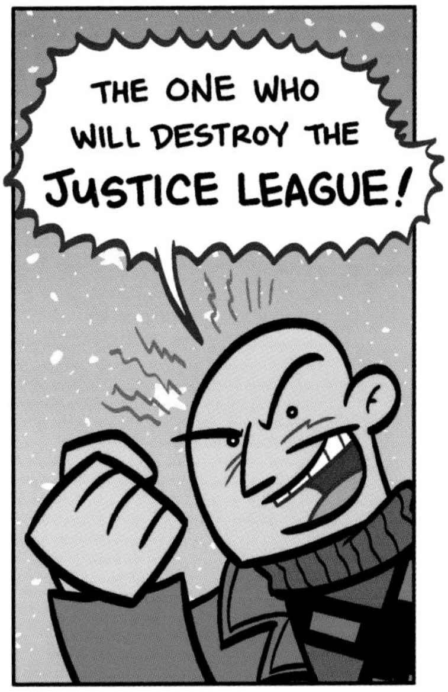
THE ONE WHO WILL DESTROY THE JUSTICE LEAGUE!

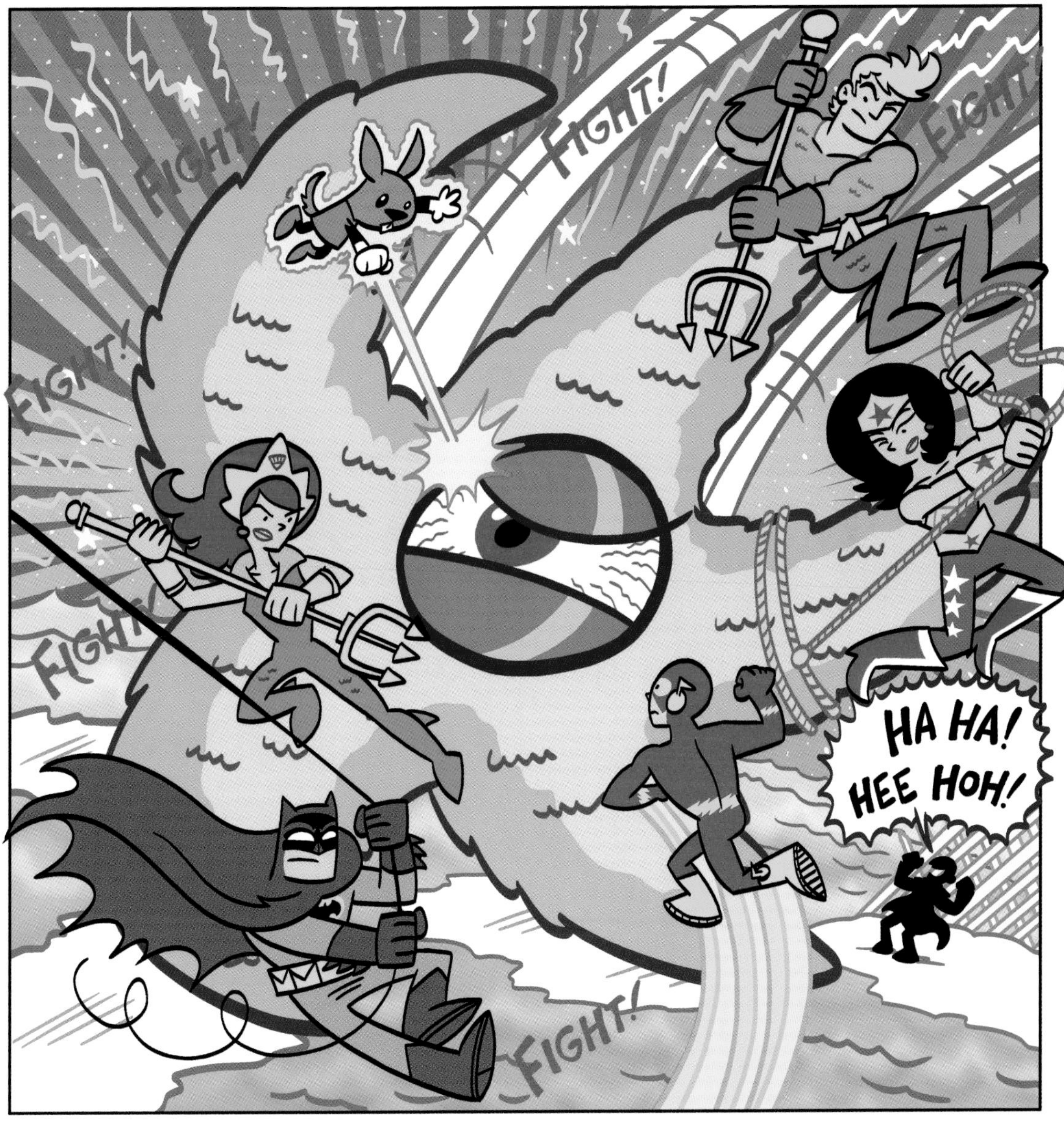
FIGHT!
FIGHT!
FIGHT!
FIGHT!
FIGHT!
FIGHT!
HA HA! HEE HOH!

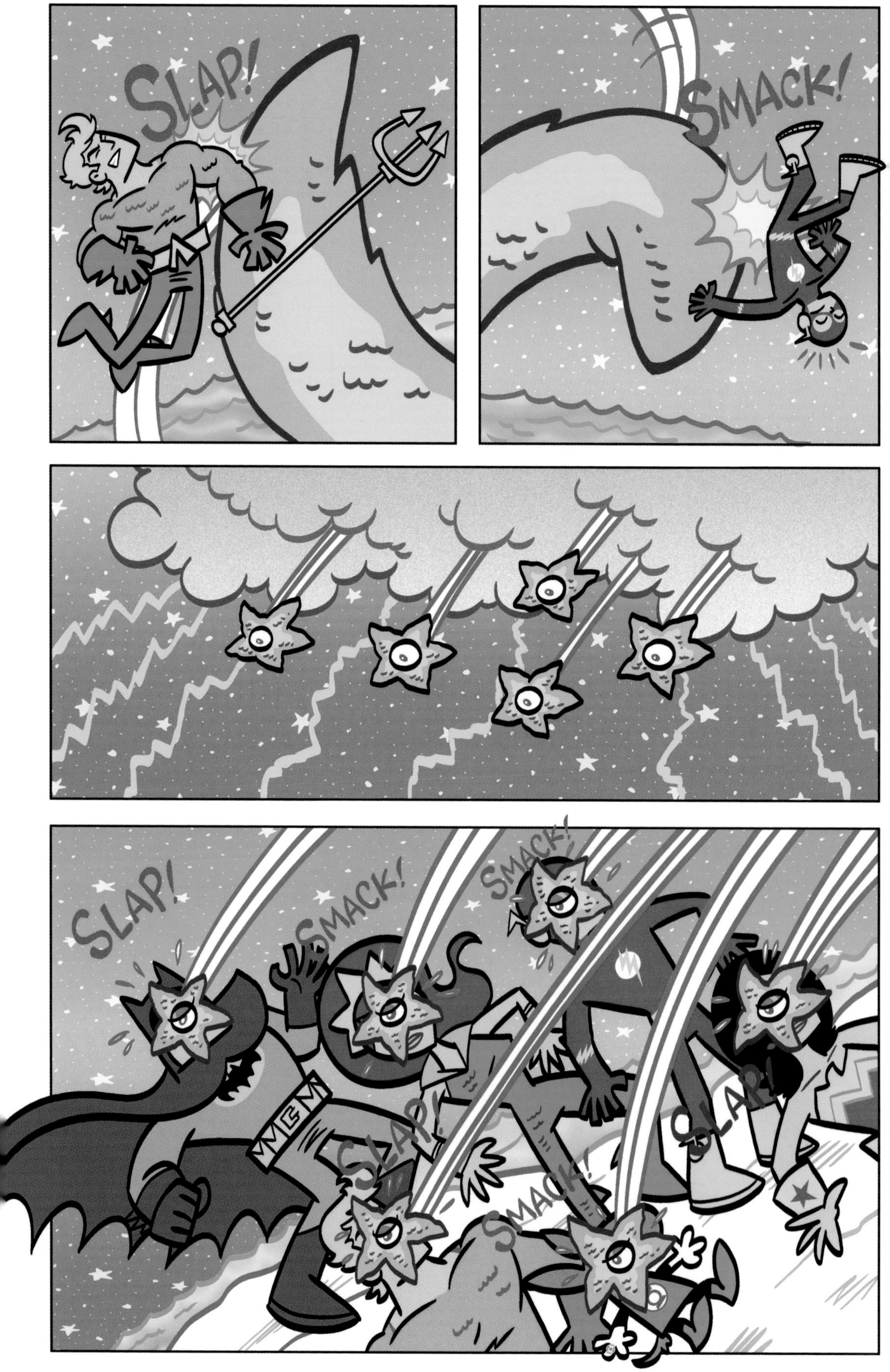
SLAP!
SMACK!
SLAP!
SMACK!
SMACK!
SLAP!
SMACK!
SLAP!

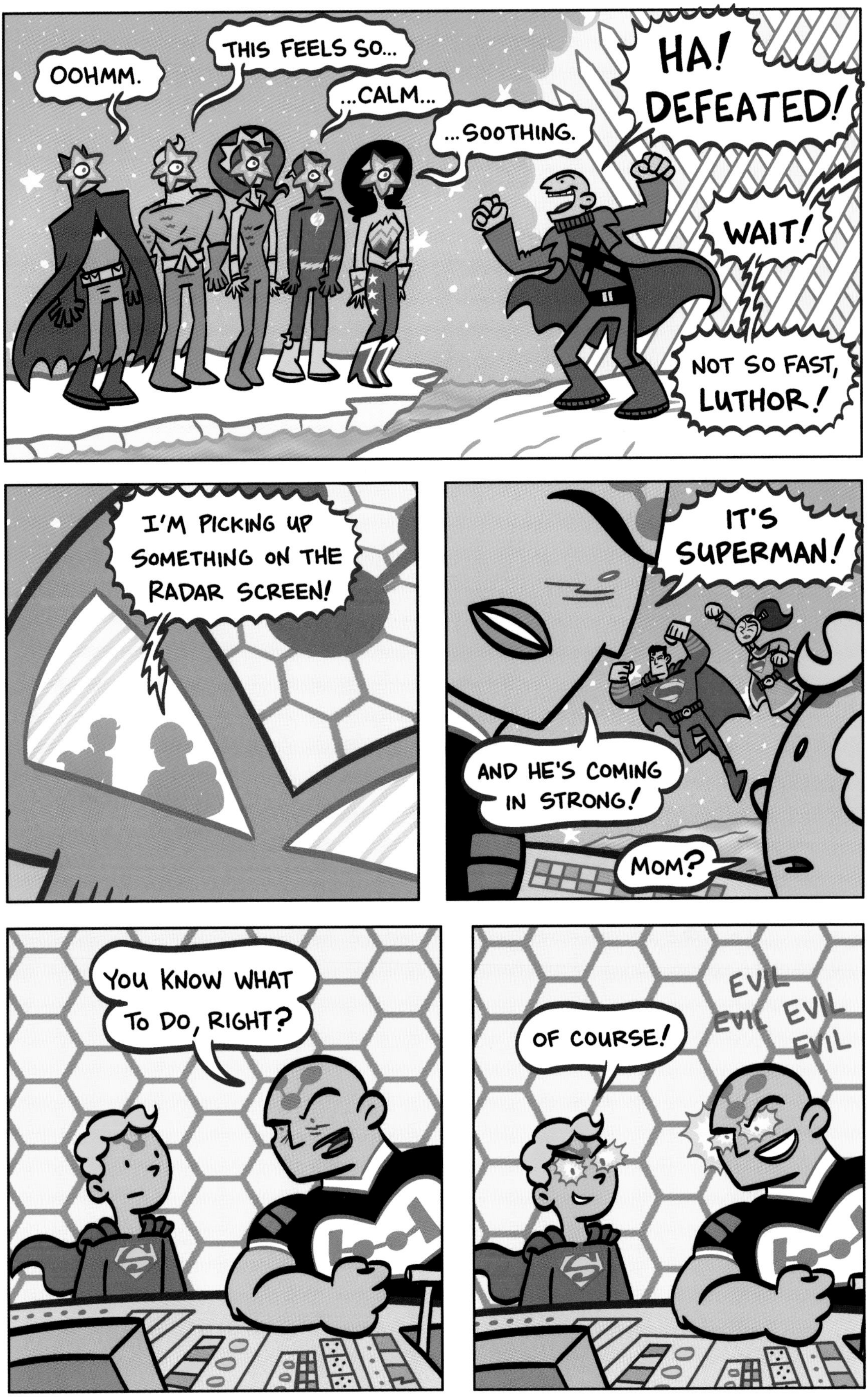
OOHMM.
THIS FEELS SO...
...CALM...
...SOOTHING.
HA! DEFEATED!
WAIT!
NOT SO FAST, LUTHOR!
I'M PICKING UP SOMETHING ON THE RADAR SCREEN!
IT'S SUPERMAN!
AND HE'S COMING IN STRONG!
MOM?
YOU KNOW WHAT TO DO, RIGHT?
OF COURSE!
EVIL EVIL EVIL EVIL

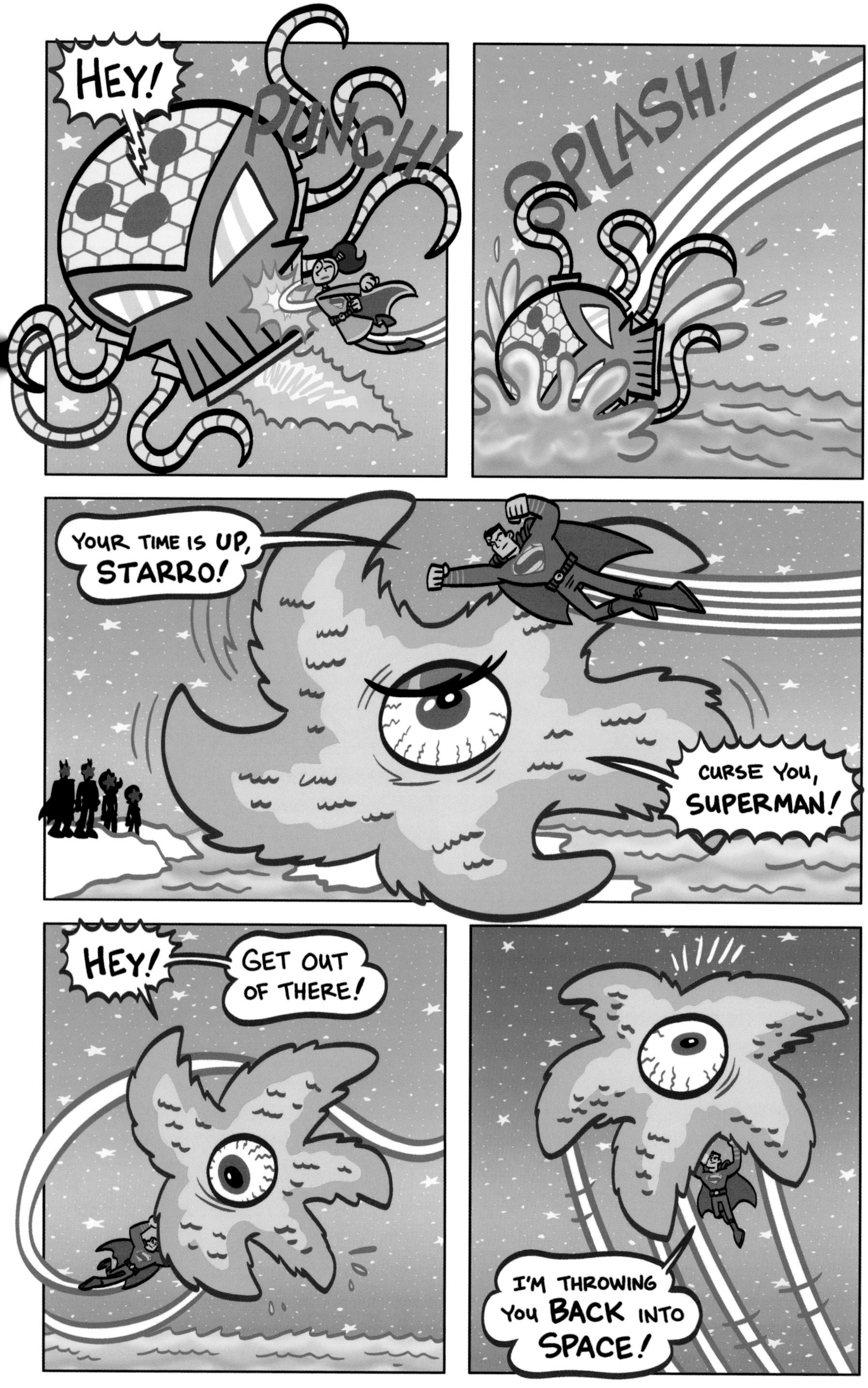
HEY!
PUNCH!
SPLASH!
YOUR TIME IS UP, STARRO!
CURSE YOU, SUPERMAN!
HEY!
GET OUT OF THERE!
I'M THROWING YOU BACK INTO SPACE!

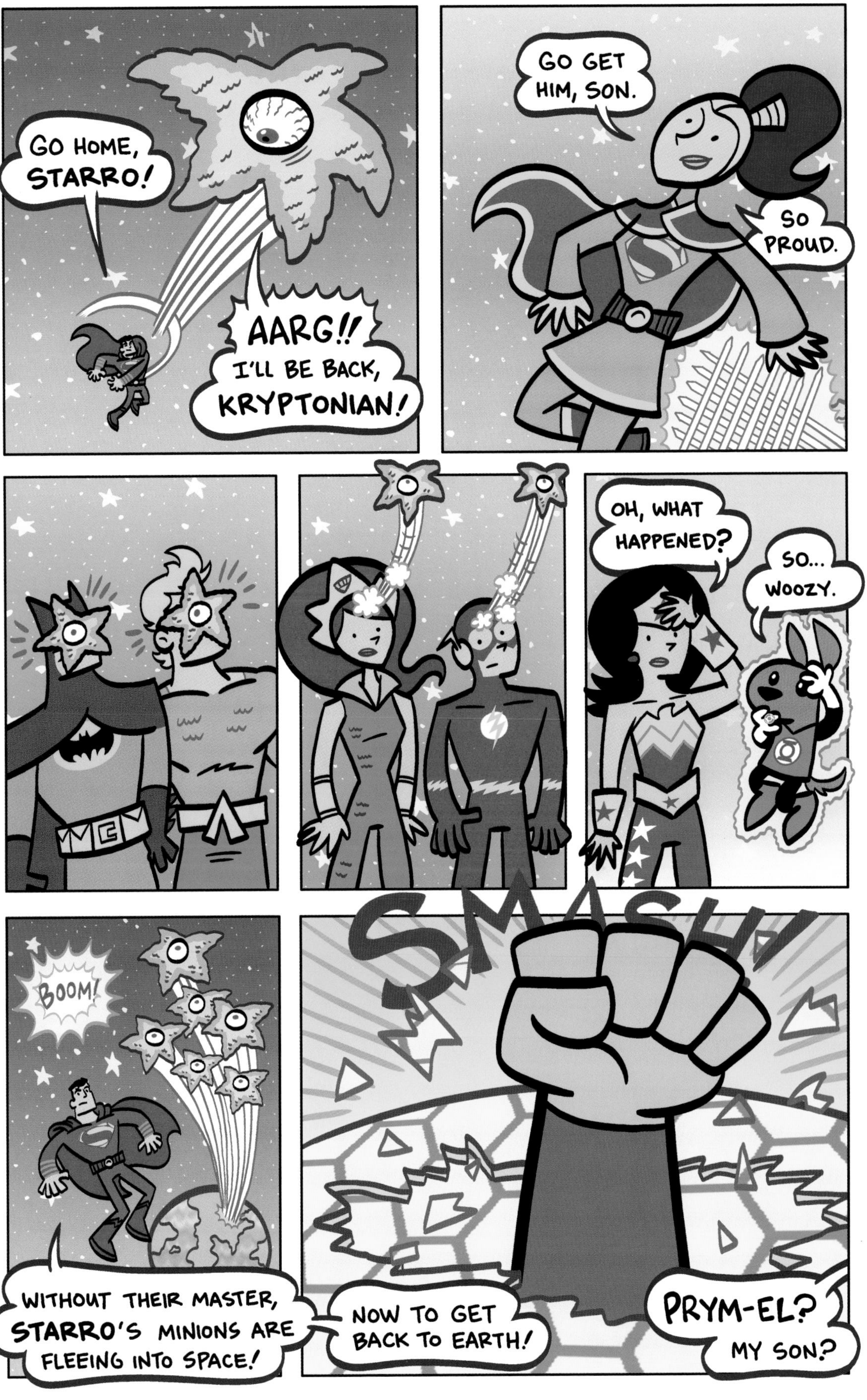
GO HOME, STARRO!
AARG!! I'LL BE BACK, KRYPTONIAN!
GO GET HIM, SON.
SO PROUD.
OH, WHAT HAPPENED?
SO... WOOZY.
BOOM!
WITHOUT THEIR MASTER, STARRO'S MINIONS ARE FLEEING INTO SPACE!
NOW TO GET BACK TO EARTH!
SMASH!
PRYM-EL? MY SON?

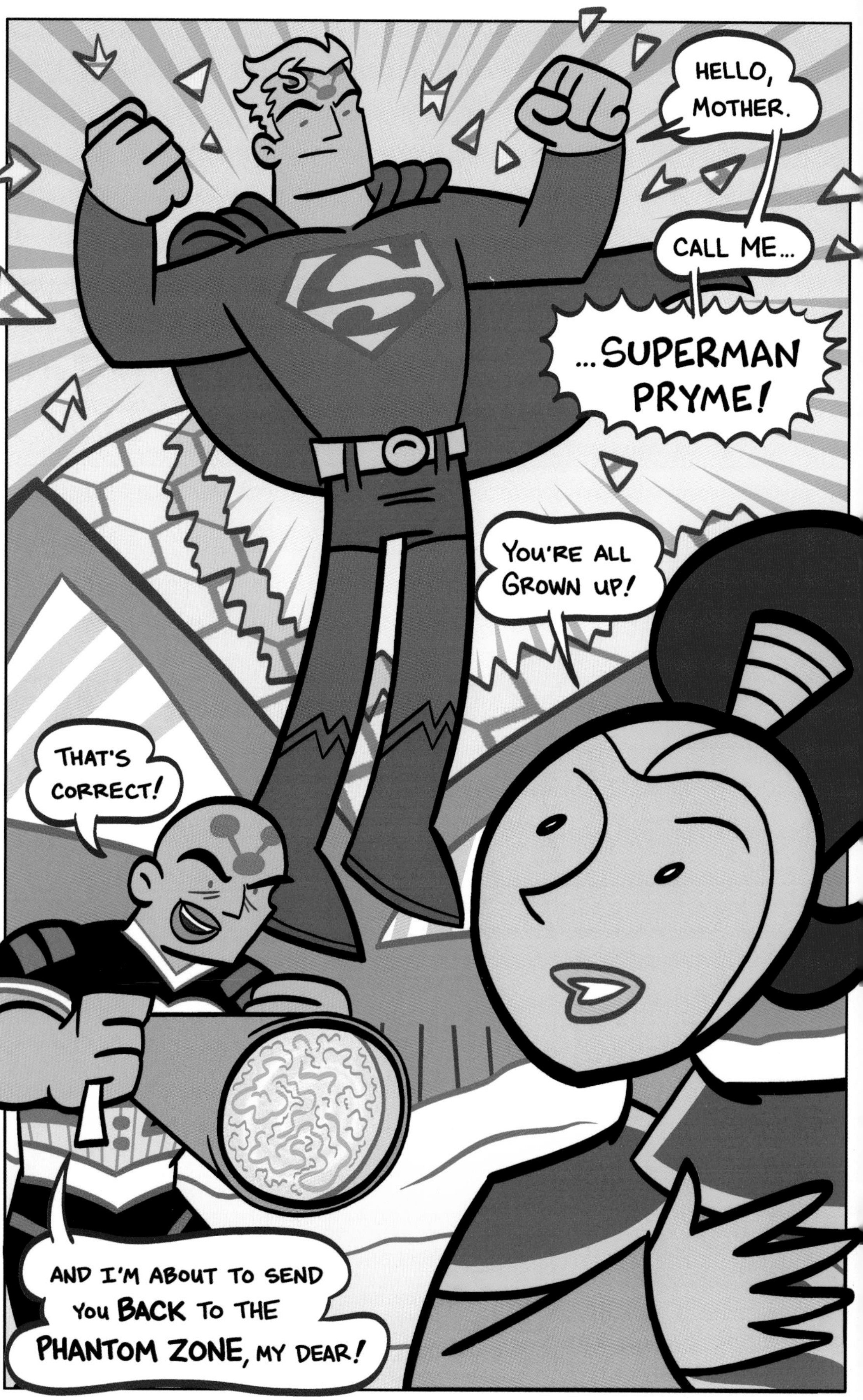
HELLO, MOTHER.
CALL ME...
...SUPERMAN PRYME!
YOU'RE ALL GROWN UP!
THAT'S CORRECT!
AND I'M ABOUT TO SEND YOU BACK TO THE PHANTOM ZONE, MY DEAR!

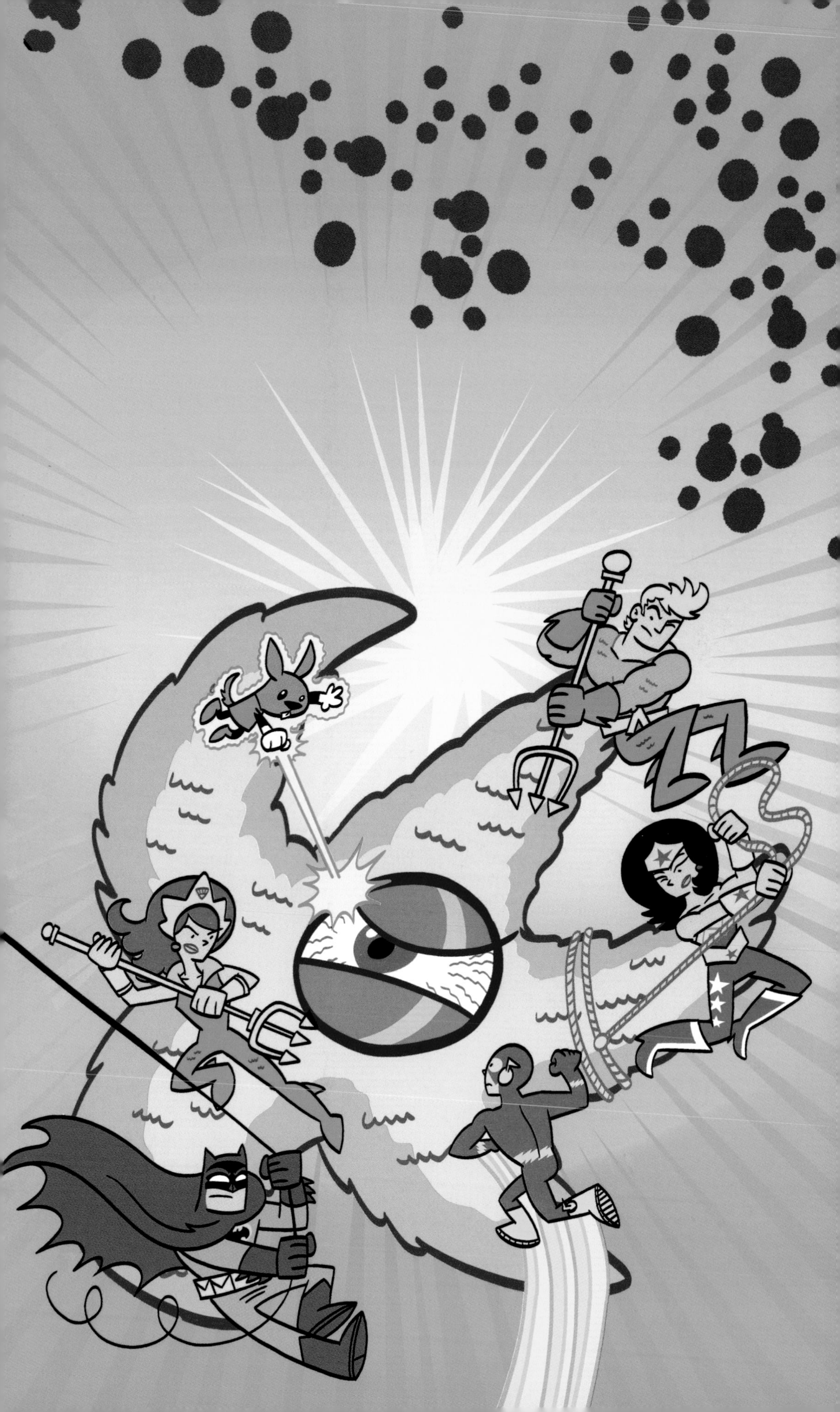

CREATORS

ART BALTAZAR IS A CARTOONIST MACHINE FROM THE HEART OF CHICAGO! HE DEFINES CARTOONS AND COMICS NOT ONLY AS AN ART STYLE, BUT AS A WAY OF LIFE. CURRENTLY, ART IS THE CREATIVE FORCE BEHIND *THE NEW YORK TIMES* BEST-SELLING, EISNER AWARD-WINNING DC COMICS SERIES TINY TITANS, THE CO-WRITER FOR *BILLY BATSON AND THE MAGIC OF SHAZAM!,* AND CO-CREATOR OF SUPERMAN FAMILY ADVENTURES. ART IS LIVING THE DREAM! HE DRAWS COMICS AND NEVER HAS TO LEAVE THE HOUSE. HE LIVES WITH HIS LOVELY WIFE, ROSE, BIG BOY SONNY, LITTLE BOY GORDON, AND LITTLE GIRL AUDREY. RIGHT ON!

ART BALTAZAR

FRANCO

FRANCO AURELIANI, BRONX, NEW YORK, BORN WRITER AND ARTIST, HAS BEEN DRAWING COMICS SINCE HE COULD HOLD A CRAYON. CURRENTLY RESIDING IN UPSTATE NEW YORK WITH HIS WIFE, IVETTE, AND SON, NICOLAS, FRANCO SPENDS MOST OF HIS DAYS IN A BATCAVE-LIKE STUDIO WHERE HE HAS PRODUCED DC'S TINY TITANS COMICS. IN 1995, FRANCO FOUNDED BLINDWOLF STUDIOS, AN INDEPENDENT ART STUDIO WHERE HE AND FELLOW CREATORS CAN CREATE CHILDREN'S COMICS. FRANCO IS THE CREATOR, ARTIST, AND WRITER OF *PATRICK THE WOLF BOY.* WHEN HE'S NOT WRITING AND DRAWING, FRANCO ALSO TEACHES HIGH SCHOOL ART.

GLOSSARY

agenda (uh-JEN-duh)—a list of things that need to be done or discussed

design (di-ZYN)—to create or build something a specific way

hologram (HOL-uh-gram)—a three-dimensional image made by laser beams

hover (HUHV-ur)—to remain in one place in the air

introduce (in-truh-DOOSS)—to bring in a new person, or to help two or more people meet

justice (JUHSS-tiss)—fair action or treatment, or when punishment is given for breaking the law

legion (LEE-juhn)—a large number of soldiers

minion (MIN-yen)—an underling, henchmen, or follower of an important person or villain

outrageous (out-RAY-juhss)—very shocking or offensive

perpetrator (PURP-uh-tray-tor)—someone who commits a certain act, usually breaking a rule or committing a crime

radar (RAY-dahr)—a device that uses radio waves to track the location of objects

riddle (RID-uhl)—a statement or question that makes you think and that often has a surprising answer

robot (ROH-bot)—a machine programmed to do jobs usually performed by a person

VISUAL QUESTIONS AND WRITING PROMPTS

1. WHAT IF BLACK MANTA DIDN'T WANT TO JOIN THE LEGION OF DOOM? WRITE WHAT HAPPENS NEXT IN THIS SCENE.

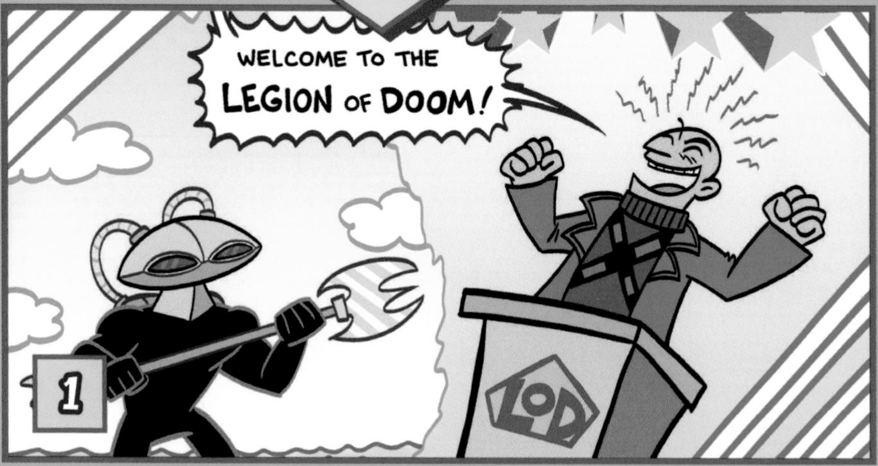
WELCOME TO THE LEGION OF DOOM!
LOD
1

2. LOOK AGAIN AT THE PANEL BELOW. WHAT DO YOU THINK THE STARFISH DID TO THE JUSTICE LEAGUE?

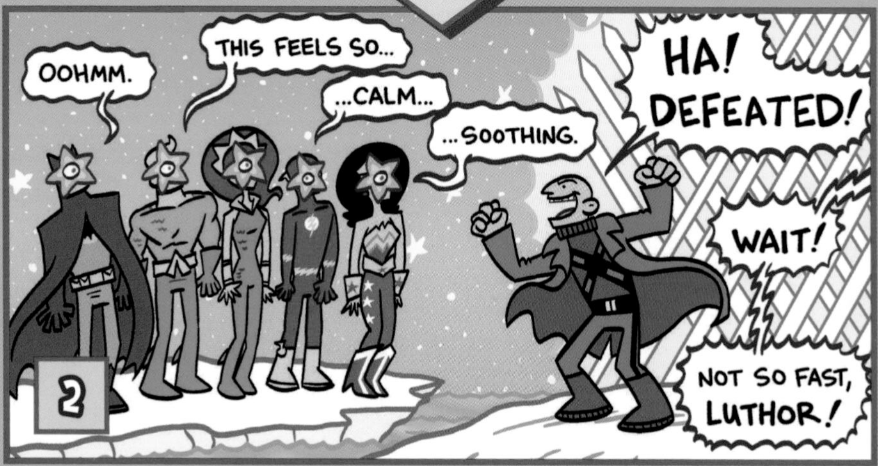
OOHMM.
THIS FEELS SO...
...CALM...
...SOOTHING.
HA! DEFEATED!
WAIT!
NOT SO FAST, LUTHOR!
2

3. WHY DO YOU THINK BRAINIAC WAITED TO ATTACK THE JUSTICE LEAGUE?

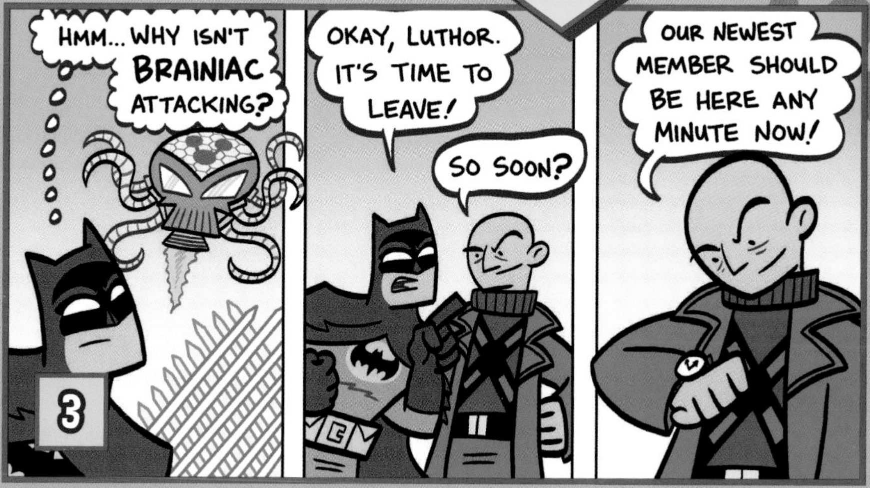
HMM... WHY ISN'T BRAINIAC ATTACKING?
3
OKAY, LUTHOR. IT'S TIME TO LEAVE!
SO SOON?
OUR NEWEST MEMBER SHOULD BE HERE ANY MINUTE NOW!

4. WHY WOULD BRAINIAC WANT PRYM-EL TO GROW INTO SUPERMAN PRYME?

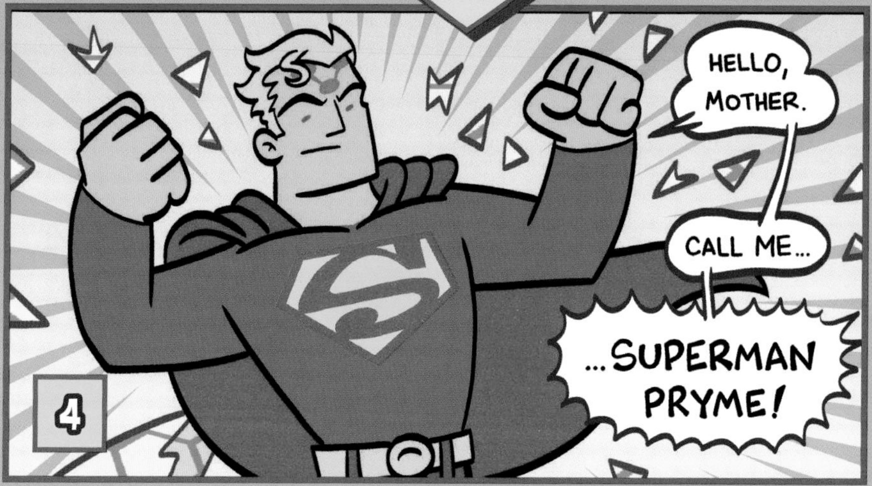
HELLO, MOTHER.
CALL ME...
...SUPERMAN PRYME!
4

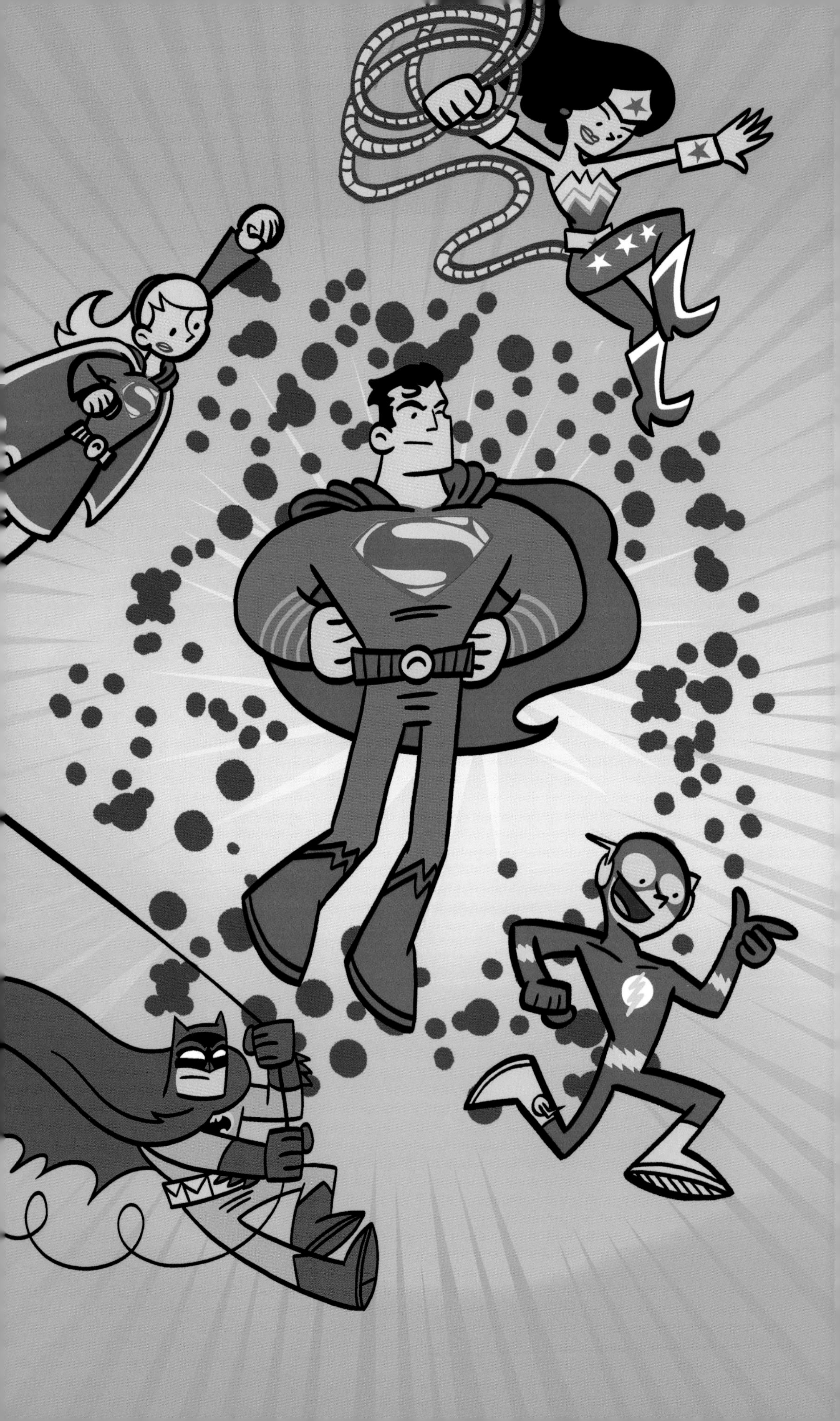

READ THEM ALL!

SUPER POWERS!
Dark Knight Dilemma!

SUPER POWERS!
Composite Crisis!

SUPER POWERS!
Brimstone Attacks!

SUPER POWERS!
League vs Legion!

SUPER POWERS!
Pryme Time!

SUPER POWERS!
The Wrath of Apokolips!

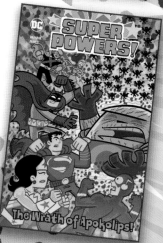

only from

STONE ARCH BOOKS

a capstone imprint

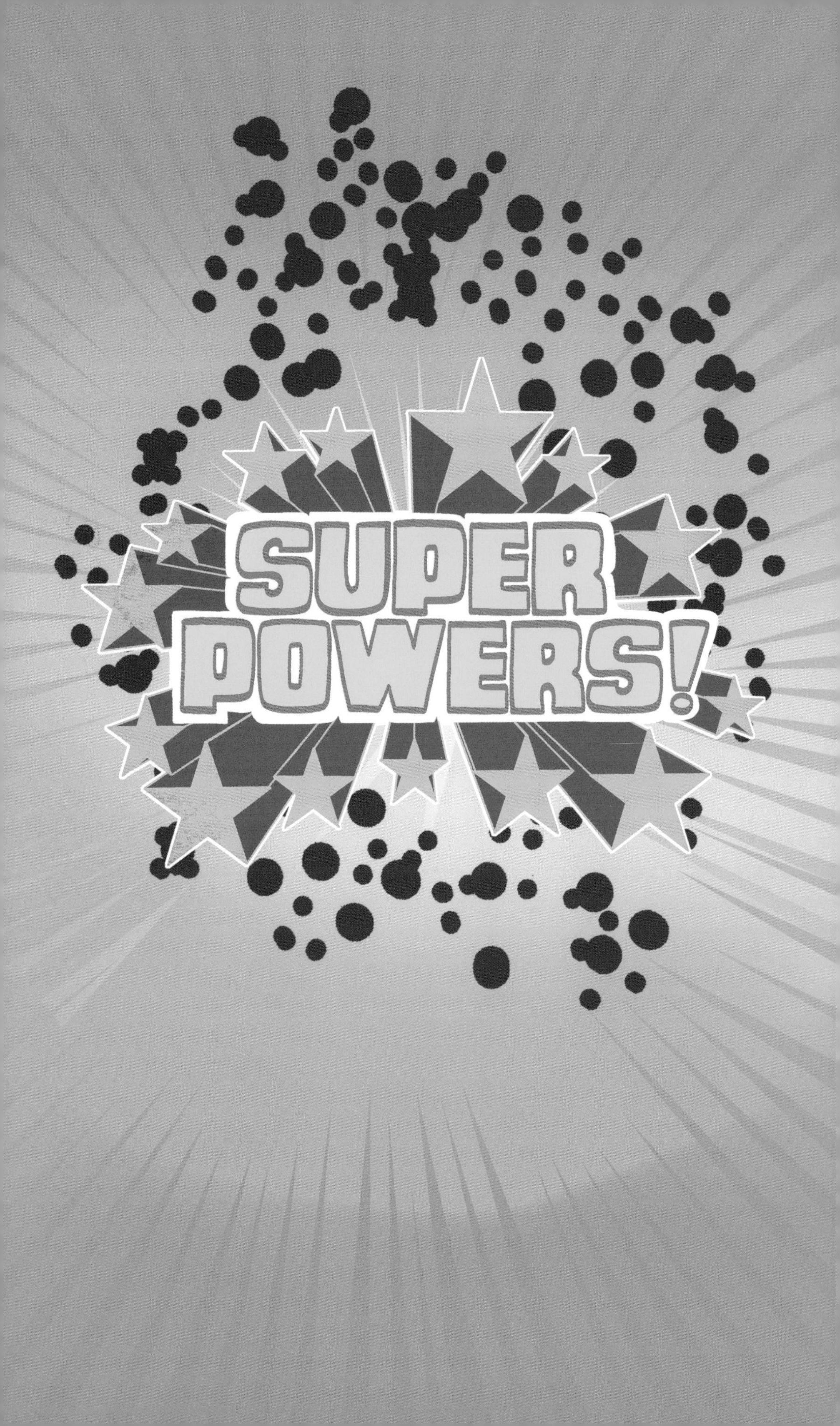
SUPER POWERS!